Impossible Appetites

The Iowa School
of Letters Award
for Short Fiction

Impossible Appetites

Nine stories by James Fetler

University of Iowa Press
Iowa City, Iowa
1980

ACKNOWLEDGMENTS

These previously published stories appeared originally in somewhat different form:
"Impossible Appetites," *Commentary* (August 1978).
"The Dust of Yuri Serafimovich," *Atlantic Monthly* (June 1966).
"The Blum Invitation," *Story* (May 1967).
"Mutability and the Meat Loaf," *Prairie Schooner* (Spring 1967).
"The Indians Don't Need Me Any More," *Literary Review* (Summer 1973).

"Watchmann's Cubes" and "All Terminations Begin in the Mind" have been accepted for publication by the *Paris Review* and appear in this collection by permission of Fayette Hickox, managing editor of the *Paris Review*.

Library of Congress Cataloging in Publication Data

Fetler, James, 1931–
Impossible appetites.

(The Iowa School of Letters award for short fiction)
I. Title. II. Series: Iowa. University. School of Letters. Iowa School of Letters award for short fiction.
PZ4.F325Im [PS3556.E473] 813'.54 80-17200
ISBN 0-87745-101-X
ISBN 0-87745-102-8 (pbk.)

University of Iowa Press, Iowa City 52242

Printed in the United States of America

FOR ANDREW FETLER AND MAXINE HAMILTON

Contents

Impossible Appetites

I

APRIL 21, 1969–JUNE 14, 1969

MONDAY. We got back to her apartment after dark and I spotted the note in the mailbox but kept my mouth shut. She drew the drapes and unbuckled my belt. I was reaching for her when she turned and went into the bathroom. The tub started splashing. She said soak and unwind for a while, and went out to the kitchen. I said Julie, there's nothing to unwind.

During dinner she kept making amusing comparisons between Telegraph Avenue today and the way it was nine years ago, before the zombies and urban guerrillas set up camp. After dinner she led me to the cot, and for about twenty minutes I felt I was being worked over by somebody else. She had never been that intense or methodical, not even when we had first met. As I was falling asleep I felt grateful to her, and my gratitude angered me.

I found the note in her jacket pocket in the middle of the night and checked the number against the Berkeley directory and crawled back to bed. Struggled out of bed at 5 A.M. and got dressed without waking her up and drove back to Palo Alto, a hammering in my head.

TUESDAY. We yelled for over an hour. I hung up. She phoned back: protestations of love, accusations, interrogations, counter-accusations, remorse. She said there's nothing between her and Thad, she's just naturally worried about him—you don't live with a man for four years and then stand back and whistle as he slides down the drain. I said it didn't exactly sound to me like the comical fellow was sliding down the drain with his sexual double-entendres. She said Joe, you don't understand him, he happens to be gifted with levity and wit. I said well, that's fantastic, you're welcome to try four more years of that vaudeville act.

FRIDAY. I had vowed not to drive up last night, but I started to pace back and forth in the carport and suddenly I opened the door to the car and took off. Arrived close to midnight, my head full of sherry and cigarette smoke. She said Christ, take a look at yourself! I kicked off my shoes and fell asleep while she was still brushing her teeth.

Struggled out of bed at 5:30 A.M., everything in slow motion, a feeling of fog hanging over the kitchen. Coffee and a handful of vitamin Cs. She said Joe, what's the matter with you, driving up glassy-eyed in the middle of the night—you're a grown man with kids—and that sherry, night after night, turns me off worse than anything else. I said Julie, no more booze. She said wow.

I reached out to her carefully. She waited for me to let go. I held her without really holding, the way I had taught myself to do when we met. She kept standing there, patiently waiting for me to back off and sit down. I kissed the rim of her ear. Finally she did her eye-roll and sighed here we go, folks! and we went to the cot.

During lunch today Sparrow said Joey, you'll burn yourself out on the Nimitz Freeway if you keep up this pace, I've never seen you as driven as this. I said mind your own business and leave me alone. He said look at the bags under your eyes. Stayed away from the sherry tonight and was careful not to phone.

WEDNESDAY. She says she appreciates being desired as much as the next person, but she can't help backing off whenever anyone grovels or leans. She says I'm asking for things she can't possibly give on demand. The moment I walk through her door I start mashing her bosom and aim for the sack. Same thing in the morning. She says how would you feel if you showed up at work every morning with a wet crotch? I suggested maybe we have different thermostats or something. She said maybe we do, Joe—just don't tamper with mine. I asked if she'd seen Thad again. She said I'm not accountable to you. Bought a new pair of boots for the trip.

TUESDAY. Mt. Shasta. She's still asleep in her bunk. There were rats in the rafters last night. Arrived at Sand Flat by noon yesterday and hiked up to the cabin without too much difficulty even though there's been lots of fresh snow. She's impressed by the view. As I was taking a close-up of her drinking water from the pump, I remembered the marvelous shot I had taken of Claire years ago, when the pump was completely encrusted in ice. I expected other hikers to be using this camp, but so far we've got the entire stone hut to ourselves.

Broiled our steaks outside last night, snow all around us, a sudden hailstorm pelting us as we bent over our pots. Julie kept whistling and uttering whimsical one-liners. She said Berkeley has turned into Mecca, everyone's so conscientiously pure and correct. I said Julie, you sound like your father again.

We built a fire in the stone hut and drank brandy, the winds rumbling up near the summit somewhere. As we sat side by side in front of the fire she kept playing with her gloves. The logs started breaking apart. She asked how many times I had been here before. I said only once, a few months after Claire had had the miscarriage. Laura was six at the time. She asked if Laura had hiked up with us. I said yes, she was way out in front most of the way. Julie said well, you were certainly cruel to Claire, weren't you, running after those students of yours and then letting her get pregnant again—do you always return to the scene of the crime? I said hey, you don't know what you're talking about, better leave it alone! We finished the brandy. She lit another cigarette.

She said as far back as she could remember everyone had always been forcing her to try to become something she couldn't possibly be. The first months with Thad had been carefree and light—he clowned around like you wouldn't believe and they laughed all the time, it was great. But then Thad started changing, the same as the others, he became more demanding and moody and snapped and grew sullen and stayed out very late, often drinking with friends or driving around by himself aimlessly, and finally it got into yelling and physical blows.

I said boy, I can't comprehend how you took it so long. She said yeah. I threw another log on the fire and climbed up to my bunk. I watched her sitting there, flicking the cigarette ashes into the fireplace, and realized it wasn't her arms I was hungering for.

II

AUGUST 18, 1969–SEPTEMBER 19, 1969

MONDAY. Attached the shutters to the turret windows this morning. Julie finished upholstering the chairs. The plants in the alcove are doing surprisingly well, considering the heat. Finished painting the sun porch last night. Julie said the Victorians had their faults, but they certainly knew how to put up a civilized house—the Victorians wouldn't tolerate aluminum-frame windows. I said they didn't have aluminum. She said that's not the point, Joe.

Laura phoned, very distraught. Two more baby rabbits chewed up by some cat. Drove to Hopkins Street and examined the hutch. I couldn't find any tunnels or holes, but it's obviously going to require a plywood floor. Alex rode up on his tricycle and stared at the matted fur on the grass. I carried him into the house. Claire brewed some coffee and reminded me for the fourth time that she never wanted the rabbits in the first place—this was part of a regular pattern with me. I spotted one of the neighborhood cats slinking along the fence and threw the coffee cup at it. Claire said well, I can see that your girl friend is bringing out the best in you these days, and went into the house. Laura sat next to me on the back steps and clung to my arm for a while. We buried the rabbits in the vegetable patch. Julie seemed tense when I finally came home.

FRIDAY. Laura helped me rebuild the hutch yesterday. Put in a solid plywood floor. I was getting ready to climb up on the roof to adjust the TV antenna when Claire grabbed my ankle and said never mind, I got tired of waiting for you to adjust it—Rex is coming over in half an hour with his toolbox. I said since when do you need a toolbox to adjust an antenna? She let go of my ankle and went back inside. Gave Laura her allowance and left.

Julie had flowers in bowls everywhere. We sat in the alcove and worked out the itinerary. The afternoon sun was striking the chandelier and the ceiling was quivering with diamond shapes. She put her hair up for dinner and wore her Henry James blouse. We dined at opposite ends of the massive mahogany table, separated by flowers and candles. The game hens she had fixed were exquisite. Wild rice and chablis. After the second glass of wine she sat back and said this is more like it, isn't it? I said it certainly beats that cramped studio apartment off the Bayshore Freeway. She said boy, you were drinking a lot in those days, weren't you. I said well, leaving a wife and two kids isn't exactly an easy adjustment to make. She said maybe I'm different from you: when I see that it's time to get moving, I just swallow two aspirins and move. I said it wasn't exactly like that when you ran into Thad. She said listen to you! You are hardly the person to talk!

I tried coaxing her to the couch after dinner but she pushed me away. She said she needed to work on her renderings for a while. I said fine. I went into the alcove and tried reading Ouspensky. She crashed around midnight. I sat in the alcove with the sherry decanter and tried to figure her out. Around one I climbed into the car and drove past Hopkins Street. The lights were out and the 4-wheel drive Toyota was parked behind Claire's Maverick. I headed up the Bayshore as far as Coyote Point and looked at the boats for a while and drove home.

TUESDAY. Sparrow was very excited: he's lined up an ex-Jesuit from Brazil who suggests that Julie and I compose our own script. Creative spirituality. I told Julie I was swamped with paperwork—could she come up with something. She said sure, and she promised not to include anything by my father or Kahlil Gibran.

FRIDAY. Got the traveler's checks. Puzzled over Julie's script: excerpts from Bob Dylan and Teilhard de Chardin and a big chunk of Rilke. Drove up to the Fortress for prime rib and broccoli. Mrs Bronson was gracious and strained. During dinner the Commander inquired if I had reservations for all of the stops. I assured him I did. And I got the car finally tuned? Yes, I got the car finally tuned. How much did they charge me to get the car tuned? I told him how much. He said well, that's all right. He asked if the tires were still good. I said the tires are still pretty good. After dinner Mrs Bronson passed around sticks of sugarless gum on a small silver tray. I took Julie aside and said listen, do you think I should let him examine my teeth? She gave me her watch-your-step smile.

She remained up on the hill for the night. I drove home and began sorting piles of old letters. Trimmed my hair a little as a gesture to the Commander. Tried reading some more of Ouspensky: he says man is a lying animal. I went back to the letters. I re-read Claire's frantic notes and was hit with remorse. I kept thinking about the way I had shaken her off like a bur. I glanced at my journals of ten years ago. Hungers, predictions and plans.

MONDAY. Portland. Julie is twitching under the blankets again. Her stomach is still bothering her. Spent the afternoon roaming about on the bluffs by myself.

Saturday started out humid and warm. The Brazilian ex-Jesuit turned out to be a typical Sparrow maneuver—a psychic healer from the Church of the Internal Divine. Massive rings on each finger and a cloth over his head. The Bronsons strove mightily to be cordial and correct, but they couldn't disguise their chagrin. Julie was effervescent and showed me off to the clan. Got into a brief dialogue with the uncle who is a mortician in Bakersfield. He said I want you and Julie to come down and visit us soon. I said well, we certainly will. During the ceremony Laura withdrew to the rear of the garden. Alex clung to my knee. Julie's sister strummed her guitar.

As soon as it was over Sparrow came up to me and I saw there were tears in his eyes. He said Joe, I'm so happy for you! I wanted to assure him that all the terrible yearning was now in the past, but his wife started hugging me and the guests milled around and there wasn't time for words. When Laura came up to congratulate us I got the impression she was glaring at me. The Commander's aerospace people lumbered into the dining room for the buffet. Mrs Bronson was smiling nonstop and seemed tight as a drum. Sparrow, Sol Luken and Mandel slipped away to the apricot orchard with the Brazilian. Their wives gathered up their children and left. They were still passing around joints under the trees when Julie and I finally left to drop off the kids.

Claire offered us coffee and gave me a kiss on the cheek. Rex shook my hand vigorously: he was helping her paint the laundry room. Julie stared silently at the photographs on the living room walls.

Steady driving all day yesterday, Julie reading travel guides on Seattle and British Columbia. She said wow, Sparrow's wife has turned into a dumpy little thing, hasn't she.

Stopped in Ashland last night: a decaying motor court with stone dwarfs and little windmills on poles. The radiator overheated today, steam hissing up at the windshield. Got it fixed at a rural garage at the foot of some beautiful hills. We sat in the mechanic's dark office for a couple of hours drinking Dr Pepper and reading *Field and Stream*. When I tried putting my arm around her, she said Joe, can't you see I'm not feeling very well. I said sorry and went out to look at the hills.

THURSDAY. Orcas Island, Puget Sound. Brilliant water and keen blasts of wind. The old hotel seems deserted—I think we're the only guests here. Our room has a view of the Sound. I watched the ferry come in before dinner tonight. The bed creaks. There's one chair. On the night stand, a pitcher and basin. The toilet down the hall makes funereal sounds.

SATURDAY. Victoria, B.C. The Empress is an impressive old pile. We had tea in the lobby but had little to say. When I tried to maneuver her to bed before dinner she said she wanted to soak in the tub for a while and read up on the history of this area. I said it has quite a history. She said that's what I've heard.

I went down to the lobby, looked around, converted some of my money into Canadian currency to reinforce the illusion that I was abroad, spent an hour in the bar, wandered over to the buildings of Parliament: hundreds of light globes like a theatrical set. Started thinking about Claire and the children. In a setting like this, Claire would be resting her head on my chest. When I got back to our room Julie was twitching in her sleep.

This morning I tried catching her on film. She pretended to ignore me. When I tried to pursue her on the deck of the ferry with the movie camera, she lunged at me. I jerked the camera back. She hesitated, then laughed.

WEDNESDAY. Palo Alto. The Oregon coastline kept shifting from sharp precipices to pockets of gray. As soon as we headed into the mountains the car started steaming again. She said you should've listened to my father, Joe. I didn't say anything. She said he warned you about the water pump. We gave up on Mt Lassen and drove straight to Tahoe, the car chugging worse as the altitude increased.

The casinos at Tahoe were running around the clock like huge vending machines. I followed Julie from table to table and tried fathoming her gambling technique. She was all calculation and internal strategy. She said she had learned all the tricks by observing her father when she was a girl. I said well, I'm sure the Commander is a fabulous poker player—he's got a face like a cement wall. She ignored that and went to the roulette tables. The smoke in the casino bothered my eyes, but her luck held up well and we managed to get two complimentary drinks. She was still playing roulette at 3:30 A.M. I was hungry and went to the coffee shop for some terrible scrambled eggs. Styrofoam. I propped myself up in a chair in the lobby and slept for a while.

This morning I asked her how she felt about her father. She smiled politely at me, a bad sign. I said look, I'm just curious—I've never seen you two close, but you seem to have some kind of bond. She said Joe, all this heavy introspecting simply keeps you from getting on top of yourself.

III

SEPTEMBER 25, 1969–OCTOBER 26, 1969

THURSDAY. She brushes her teeth, I brush mine. We put the decanter and the ashtrays away. I follow her into the bedroom. She sits on the bed in her red Chinese robe. I count the turns as she winds the alarm. She offers me her most recent analysis of Sparrow. A commonplace mind. Sparrow's deepest convictions are all platitudes. His natural impulse is to trivialize difficult things. I suggest there is more to Rod Sparrow than that, and try shifting from Sparrow to somewhat more delicate terrain. She says Joe, I am struck by the fact that you have a long history of throwing your lovers and friends to the sharks, but you keep your hooks in them and occasionally reel them in—isn't that how it usually goes? It's as though you retain little pieces and bits for some enigmatic future use. I say Julie, I've never thrown lovers and friends to the sharks. She says you're a hungry man, Joe.

I watch her. She slips out of her robe and flicks off the light. All evening she's been glittering from one room to the other, leaving her scent everywhere, and now suddenly comes the great *phew!* as she falls down the bottomless shaft. I try closing my eyes. They refuse to stay closed. I stare up at the ceiling. The patterns of passing headlights.

Finally she's asleep. I slip into my Levis and go for a walk. A patrol car drives past and slows down and goes on. Dogs start barking. A black labrador runs towards me. I pick up a section of brick from the edge of a yard. The black labrador backs away.

FRIDAY. The Bronsons dropped by after their 36 holes and suggested drapes for the flat, either eggshell or plum, they'd lend grace to the home. I agreed that drapes would certainly give the home elegance and grace. Julie said plum-colored drapes would transform the flat into a bordello. The Commander glanced at the petitions on my desk and informed me that only the top echelons are aware of what's happening in the rice paddies these days—I could hardly presume to match the intelligence-gathering capability of the Secretary of State. I said well, I'm sure you're aware that statistics are frequently juggled on every side. They measured the windows and left.

Finished fixing up the back room for Laura and Alex. Juli hasn't mentioned either of them recently and I'm trying tc ease them in more diplomatically this time. I told Laura to stop calling Julie The Governess, it isn't helping the over-all picture at all.

TUESDAY. Moratorium Day. Organized one of the teach-ins around Pentagon self-deception and statistical mirages. Sparrow was in the cafeteria circulating petitions with Luken and Mandel. Their wives were stencilling fists onto shirts. Highway Patrol appeared briefly, then faded from sight.

I walked over to the crowd that was assembling in the square and someone pulled on my shoulder and I found myself holding the mike. I climbed up on the platform and said a few words about the Geneva Convention. The crowd was responsive. I talked for ten minutes and found myself gradually modulating my voice, watching my timing, and as I was going full blast about the realities of search & destroy Sparrow appeared and announced we were going to seal off the Dumbarton Bridge on the Menlo Park side. We piled into cars and drove down to the bridge, but the sheriff was there in full force. We went back to the campus and stayed until dark. A few windows got pinged. Someone sprayed the door to the chemistry lab with red paint.

When I finally came home, Julie blinked at my armband and asked who was dead.

SUNDAY. Rich Parks had us over for dinner last night in his Japanese retreat in Los Trancos Woods. Sliding panels and mats. Julie pretended to be greatly intrigued and kept poking around with a bit too much zeal. Bev wore her hair in a single long braid and served pieces of squid with some kind of bean paste. As they talked about *satori* and Hakuin's *koan* (one hand clapping) I found myself drifting into a mist. Julie covered for me, coming up with significant questions about the wisdom of insecurity and the mirror of the mind, but I couldn't get rid of the blank. Before we departed we formed a close circle and hummed *Om* for a while. Bev dug her fingernails into my wrist. My foot fell asleep.

Julie's face flattened out as we were driving home. She said Joe, you were swaying about on your mat like some pathetic retard while that woman exhaled her fishy fumes in your ear. I said Bev didn't exhale anything in my ear, what's the matter with you, and the blankness increased.

I set myself up for experiments. The junkyard expands.

IV

NOVEMBER 21, 1969–JANUARY 6, 1970

FRIDAY. Laura has been dropping in after school while Julie is still at work, and we talk. Alex comes over on alternate weekends and says he has dreams about pigs under his bed. Julie has been civil to them. She's been taking great pains with the plants in the alcove. She's even reconciled herself to the plum-colored drapes. Our dinners are solemn rituals. We hardly ever go out. After dinner I withdraw to the sun porch with my briefcase. She sits before the fire and works on her blueprints or watches TV. She has almost completely stopped needling me about Claire. The phone rarely rings. The formality eases the strain.

THURSDAY. In the middle of the dinner today the Commander began delivering a few observations on Thanksgiving—about the deeper significance of this day. He advised us to count our blessings each day, we've been showered with physical and spiritual nourishment. Mrs Bronson kept her smile nailed to her jaw and agreed with her husband that we had a great deal, all of us, to be thankful for.

I kept pouring myself more riesling. When I carried some dishes to the kitchen Julie whispered: You're one hell of a host—don't you know how to *talk?* Kevin recalled their last trip to the Islands, and the dirt bikes they'd brought to the beach. The Commander observed that some people constantly focus on the dark side of life because they cannot be happy with what they've got. Janis recalled how her tennis game had improved in the Islands—she and Kevin had hit the courts every morning at seven, and she'd worn out two pairs of Adidas and was starting to wear out a third. I excused myself and went into the kitchen and slipped out the back door. Spent a couple of hours drinking beer in the Goose. When I came home everybody had left.

SUNDAY. As I was cleaning out the hutch yesterday—Laura's afraid to go into it now—I found the remains of four newly-born rabbits in one of the tunnels. They looked like stiff mice.

Julie was ominously controlled when I came home. She said there'll always be Hopkins Street strapped to your back—you can hardly exist without Claire and her unending chores, you're so loaded with guilt. I pushed her aside and went down to the basement with the tools. I'm building the children a puppet theater like the one we had in the gazebo when we were kids.

TUESDAY. Julie says every time she looks into my eyes she sees hunger and need, it's like Berkeley all over again. If I want her respect I will have to stop limping with my tail between my legs. I said Jesus, let's hope that it isn't like Berkeley all over again.

SATURDAY. Borrowed Sparrow's hot splicer last night and assembled the film clips of Julie. She came down to the basement and watched as I finished the editing. I left the film on the work table. An hour later it was twisted and torn, but I managed to salvage almost half of the reel.

MONDAY. Yesterday morning she's cheerful and fixes me poached eggs on muffins. Not a word about the film. We go through the Sunday paper. She says the Sunday papers aren't what they used to be. She gets up and waters the plants.

She drives off after lunch. I wander through the flat, smoke a few cigarettes, stretch myself out on the couch, get up again and stare out the window. A cat is sitting in the middle of the street. I try to read *Scientific American*. I throw the magazine down.

Julie phones: she'll be staying for dinner at the Fortress. Her sister is there with the prospective son-in-law. I say give them my love. I sit at the typewriter but don't feel like touching the keys. Claire and the children are out for the day. The *Fledermaus* on the radio irritates me.

I go to bed before eleven. I'm already half-asleep when she finally comes home. She kicks off her shoes, a bad sign. I can hear her pulling the bureau drawers open and then slamming them shut. She goes out to the kitchen, then comes back to the bedroom and lights up a cigarette and smokes in the dark.

THURSDAY. We were standing in the checkout line at the Safeway yesterday when she gave me a shove. I said hey, what's with you? She said Joe, you keep staring at me and I don't like it. I said I'm not staring at you. She hunched up her shoulders and said Christ, I can't breathe any more, you are using up my space! I threw the car keys on the checkout counter and walked home.

Christmas was quiet. The puppet theater is a success. Laura started to work on a script. Julie went drinking with the gang from the office last night. I sat in the sun porch and puzzled my way through the journals again. Impossible appetites. When she finally came home she was pretty far gone and went into the alcove and cried for a while, but we didn't discuss it.

TUESDAY. Beef brochettes with Janis & boy friend at his Tiburon dockside apartment. The developers have rechristened the place Terrapin Cove. Everywhere you look, there are tennis courts and tans. Janis said they would probably get married in the fall. Julie said what's the rush. Kevin said the Commander is squirming because his sweet daughter is living in sin. Julie said let him squirm. We broiled the brochettes on the deck of the catamaran. Julie got into a light mood and cracked jokes. As we were eating I found myself staring across Richardson Bay. I remembered that Claire and I had sailed to this cove years ago, long before there was anything here. Kevin kept mixing us hefty gin tonics. He said Joe, here's some lead for your pencil. Julie made a long face and crossed herself.

When the wind began blowing we took the gin into the cabin and watched a winter sports special on the portable TV. Kevin said he wanted to get some new scuba diving gear—they were going down to Baja next month. They talked to Julie about the kind of house they had in mind for themselves. She suggested they look at some lots in the Walnut Creek hills. Kevin asked me what kind of tires I had on the car. I said I didn't really know. He said Joe, you should really switch to steel-belted radials. I said okay, I'll look into it.

It got cold on the catamaran. As they were going back to the apartment to light the logs in the fireplace Kevin said he would take me duck-hunting one of these days. I said fine. Julie said save your money, he isn't the type. I said I'd sleep on the catamaran. Kevin dug out a down mummy bag and a pillow. Julie said don't rock the boat.

I lay in the bag for a couple of hours. I couldn't sleep. I could hear Kevin's Joan Baez tapes. A hammering came over my eyes. Around midnight I squirmed out of the bag and threw up into the bay.

V

JANUARY 7, 1970–APRIL 27, 1970

WEDNESDAY. Another dead rabbit on the grass. I still can't find any openings or underground holes. Laura doesn't go to the back yard any more.

During lunch Sparrow took me aside. He said Joe, the department is baffled by you. I said what's the complaint? He said well, you're not functioning any more—I've watched you contract steadily for the last two, three years, but your negative output has suddenly shifted to high. I said lay off the mind dynamics, you write some god-awful scripts for yourself. He said being your friend is the most difficult thing I have done in my life.

Julie has come down with the flu. I sit on the edge of the bed as she's sipping her tea. I can see her jaw working, as though I had deliberately transmitted the virus to her. She says this is the worst possible time to get sick, I'm literally swamped at work! I say they're only houses, Julie, let them wait. She says what are you talking about. Silence. She looks at me and says I've been trying my best, Joe—I've been trying to meet you halfway, even more than halfway, but I simply can't turn myself into whatever it is that you want me to be. I say Julie, I'm not trying to get you to be anything. She says Joe—you're impossible, Joe! I place my hand on her foot. She pulls her foot back.

MONDAY. During dinner she said will you kindly stop staring at me—I'm getting really annoyed by your sorrowful stares. I got up from the table and went to the front porch and stared at the houses and wondered what's happening there.

TUESDAY. Steady drizzle all morning. I don't know what I'm trying to track down. Sparrow said yesterday that my breath smelled bad.

THURSDAY. She says things worked best between us in that studio apartment off the Bayshore Freeway. She could drop in whenever the feeling was right between us, and then leave. At least we had ventilation. But when the distance was no longer there, the air got harder and harder to breathe. By the time she had moved back to Berkeley she felt practically cornered by me. This had happened with Thad and the others—it wasn't anything new. When a man slipped his arm around her waist, she felt suddenly confined. Every bed she had shared was too narrow. A man's hand on the back of her neck felt like a clamp. She was as hungry for affection as anyone else, but she couldn't exist without space. And besides, it was hard to get close to me when she smelled Hopkins Street on my shirt all the time. In my hair.

I promised to give her the distance she needs. I said I'd sleep on the cot in the sun porch. She looked hurt and relieved.

SUNDAY. I'm working in the yard when the telephone rings. Julie talks to her sister for a while. She hangs up and assures me I don't have to go up to the Fortress with her, but it's clear I'm expected to go. I change my shirt and we go.

The patio is decorated with a profusion of fresh flowers, and the Commander is wearing plaid shorts. He is offering explanatory comments about each of the wines. The aerospace people are laughing and having a marvelous time. Kevin is making predictions about the recreational vehicle industry. He says things are really starting to move in that neck of the woods. Mrs Bronson appears bringing crackers and several kinds of cheese. I compliment her on the little wine cups she had just fired in her ceramics class: the glaze matches the greenish-blue of her eyes. She pats my cheek. Julie and Janis are rummaging through their old closets upstairs.

Kevin motions me into the Commander's den. We go in. He sits on the edge of the desk. He says Joe, this is just between us: in two or three years the back roads of this country will be filled with RVs, it'll be stupendous. He sets the globe on the desk twirling. The time for the perceptive investor to make his moves is right now, Joe—we're going to see an appreciable spurt.

MONDAY. The Bronsons asked us to join them at Stanford Memorial Church to observe Easter Sunday. We went.

Kevin and Janis were there. The solemnity hung over us like cologne. I hadn't counted on brunch after the service. Julie said well, Easter brunch is traditional with them. Locked up the car with the baskets for Laura and Alex and rode up to San Francisco in Kevin's new Mercedes sedan. At the St Francis the Commander delivered a few pregnant thoughts on the subject of rededication and rebirth. He said World War II taught me that personal fulfillment is assured when the mission becomes more important than the man. We experience rebirth, he explained, when we think about others instead of just ourselves.

Janis announced they had finally fixed on a firm wedding date in September. The Commander pumped Kevin's hand and welcomed him into the family. Julie made a peculiar face. I shook Kevin's hand. We drove home by way of Walnut Creek so Kevin and Janis could check out a couple of lots. They didn't think much of the lots. As we were going back to the car Julie punched me in the arm and said damnit, stop staring at me!

SUNDAY. Ecology convocation all weekend. Sparrow gave a presentation with the overhead projector—an analysis of our dwindling resources. He announced that the future looks bleak. We must learn how to cultivate the oceans and harness the energy from the sun.

When Parks and wife arrived for dinner last night they looked tense, as though they'd just exchanged words. Julie was even more vivacious than usual. Over the curry she categorized different professions according to their idiosyncrasies. Every architect she's known has a thing about clean toilet bowls. Professors, on the other hand, are unable to think in straight lines, everything's like spaghetti to them. Rich was quiet as Bev rested her hand on my sleeve and explained the I Ching. We finished the first bottle of wine and began on another. Bev produced some of their home-grown weed.

Towards the end of the evening I found myself on the front porch with Bev. I was kissing the side of her neck. I could hear Julie laughing inside. Bev pressed her hand against my forehead and said oh, Joe, there's incredible energy blocked up in you! She backed off a little. The porch stretched away, and the steps seemed alarmingly steep. I reached out to her as the lemon tree started to bend.

When we went back inside Julie was explaining to Rich my perplexing design. She said Joe has developed a pattern of getting into relationships which he paralyzes and slowly dissects—it's got something to do with his need for dramatic control. Rich stared into his plate, as though something important were there. Julie reached for the sherry and said there are times when establishing meaningful contact with Joe is like trying to grab fish.

VI

MAY 14, 1970–MAY 27, 1970

THURSDAY. The Cambodian invasion has gotten everyone upset. Sparrow has been running all over the place with his cardboard box under his arm, soliciting attention and maneuvering himself for some kind of recognition that has nothing to do with this miserable war. I reconvened the Student-Faculty Relations Committee but got zero response. Sparrow explained that confrontation politics have made dialogue irrelevant. Watched a small group of students milling in front of Sol Luken's lab. Luken had barricaded the door and was giving them the fish-eye through the transom.

The Bronsons dropped by after dinner for coffee and Julie's upside-down cake. The Commander expressed great satisfaction over the President's firm action—he said he backs the Chief two hundred per cent, and the Republic will certainly honor its solemn commitments despite the petulant malcontents. I said listen, this war is a disgrace. He said Joe, you've been reading too many philosophy books—if it weren't for our boys in the field, you wouldn't be able to talk in this manner to me. Try Havana, or maybe Peking.

I went out to the Goose and had several beers and phoned Bev. She said fine, okay, come. I drove up to her place. She said Rich wouldn't be back for a while. We talked for an hour. She pulled off my shirt and gave me a massage with some fruit-flavored oils. I grabbed her. She said she'd been waiting for me, it was in her sun signs.

SATURDAY. Sparrow cornered me in the hall yesterday and demanded I monitor one of his Information Squads—they were going to take over the switchboard at noon. I started walking away. He said Joe, you're a narcissist, you are steeped in negation—as long as I've known you I've never seen you affirm anything long-range or beyond your own sphere, you're surrounded by ice and your hungers won't leave you in peace! I shook him off and went to my office and locked the door. He ran off to liberate the switchboard. I went down to the parking lot to make sure Rich's car was still there and drove up to see Bev.

Two high-powered hours in her bed. A massage on the living room rug afterwards. Then a vegetable salad with sprouts. I said I was having some twinges about Rich. She said Joe, don't have twinges—we're committed to actualizing whatever reality we happen to be in. I didn't say anything. She said Joe, you're a beautiful man. I said what's wrong between you and Rich? She said we've got too much soul-energy and not enough kinesthetic contact. Ate my bean sprouts and left. Julie gave me a look during dinner. We didn't talk.

TUESDAY. Went bike riding around old Palo Alto with Laura and Alex Saturday afternoon, Alex balancing himself on the rack behind me. We cycled past a house that had all the shades drawn, and I felt a dark rush, like a blow on the chest, but it filtered away.

Another rabbit was lying torn up in the yard. I extended the door to the hutch with some chickenwire and tacks.

WEDNESDAY. Found an orange card under my windshield wiper this morning, Bev's calligraphy, signs of the zodiac around the borders:

i am i and you are you
and my space is not your
space
and your space is not
mine, etc.

I stared at the card and began feeling cornered again.

Underground Christian Conspiracy hit the campus today: testimonials and guitars. I sat down on the grass and tried following their line. Political activism will not help, conservation of resources will not help, saving whales will not help, Rollo May will not help, abolition of poverty and war will not help—there is only one way to alleviate our hungers, and the bread of life cannot be found among men. I drove home. The Conspiracy has great zeal, but they've parceled off the Rock of Ages like a section of real estate.

More dreams last night. Around 4 A.M. I got up from my cot and went to the alcove to smoke. Julie came out of the bedroom. She looked drawn. I said go back to bed. She said you keep asking for more when there isn't any more. I said I'm not asking for more, go to bed. She said Joe, you are constantly asking for more.

The Dust of Yuri Serafimovich

1

Alexander Alexandrovich Kolodny, one of San Francisco's oldest and least prosperous dealers in used foreign books, weighed the old man's dog-eared volumes unenthusiastically, lifting them out of the rain-soaked carton with his left hand and giving them the one-eyed treatment. *Dreck!* Rain was always bad, it mildewed the covers and caused the pages to stick together, and now it had been raining without interruption for three days, and no letup in sight. Typical San Francisco winter. He felt the covers with the tips of his bony fingers, like a safecracker, and sniffed the inside pages. "Mold," he said, adjusting his glasses. He didn't want the books, he could see that at once, there was no demand for them—who wants nineteenth-century treatises on animals and bugs—they would simply take up extra space.

"No mold," the old man objected. His beard was like steel wool rusting in a kitchen sink. "A little damp, maybe, but no mold." He pressed his bandaged thumb against a volume in Russian on the wildfowl of the Ukraine. 1897. "I wouldn't be parting with this if I didn't have to eat."

Kolodny stared at the books. The books were useless, but the old man was tired and obviously in need of some cash. That bandage needed changing.

The old man lit a cigarette and immediately his beard began steaming like a pile of wet leaves. He pulled out a study of the commercial fishing industry in the Black Sea. "Georgi Melezhny spent seven years gathering the data."

They continued the half-hearted haggling, and as they

talked Kolodny kept his eyes on the old man and felt himself weakening. It was his cardinal fault, and he knew it—his wife had always pointed it out to him, and she was right. But on the other hand—an old countryman down on his luck. And that enormous, ancient coat, soaked from the rain.

"No one wants books on fish."

"There is much to be learned from a fish."

2

The water kettle in the back room began whistling. Kolodny glared at the rain as it streaked across the plate glass window. "The kettle," he said, padding between the shelves like a monk in his cloister. "Come in here."

The old man followed him to the back room.

Kolodny flipped the switch on the hot plate. "Look here, I'll be truthful with you. The books are worthless, an albatross around my neck. I'm in no position—but I'm cooking some hot soup and tea."

"The soup I don't need. My books."

"Soup first."

They faced each other like antagonists. The old man's beard quivered. Finally he gave in.

"You play chess," he said, tapping the board with his cane. He glanced around. A typical widower's room—a bed and a table with the hot plate. An old Morris chair, frayed, as though cats had scratched on it over the years. A couple of wooden chairs, the legs reinforced with wire. A cupboard. Nothing more. "You're from the south," Kolodny observed, carefully wrapping a hot pad around the handle of the spoon.

"Odessa."

"I never liked it. I was robbed in Odessa. Thirty-six years ago."

"Everyone to his taste."

3

The old man sucked up the soup noisily, wielding the

spoon with his left hand as though he were digging a hole in a flowerpot. In his eagerness to sell the books he had forgotten his hunger. Now it came. A noodle stuck to his whiskers.

As they shared the simple meal—instant soup with black bread and tall glasses of very weak tea—the two countrymen talked. The old fellow's name was Yuri Vassilyvich Serafimovich, and he had come to the end of his savings, which he had been accumulating in small lumps over the years here and there as a seaman, a prospector, a veterinarian, a gardener in a Mexican convent. He had seen the world in his day, roaming about, examining the ways of wild creatures and men.

Always there had been animals in his life. Animals were important, they explained many facts of existence. He talked about the pets he had owned. "Parakeets," he sighed. "More than one. And, dear God—monkeys and drakes, and a trained rat, a rat who slept on the pillow with me. And how many cats I don't remember. Calico and long-haired. And when I worked in the convent I had an armadillo, *Dasypus novemcinctus,* and a deer which was shot by a hungry policeman. And birds. Birds who talked. Give me more tea. I'll tell you something. There are places I went where a man does not usually venture. Do you know about the island of cats? In the Irish Sea is a great reef, off the Isle of Man, where only cats live. Cats. I row out in a skiff. I row for a long time, and then there is the reef, like a sea serpent lying on its side. Over the years the cats have grown large and ferocious. I sit in the skiff, near the edge of the reef. In the bottom of the skiff is a leak. All day I bail water and study the cats. Then the sun sets, and the moon comes, and the cats creep down to the strand and fish with their claws. I watch the cats fish."

They drank their tea in silence.

Serafimovich leaned back and studied his wet moccasins. "Look at those clubs. With those two clubs I tramped through Sonora at the time of the worst peasant revolts, when whole villages looked like butchering shambles. In Yucatán I was captured by drug-chewing insurgents who left me head-down in a pit with my dead mule. And when I was very young, hardly out of my teens, I crept into the Potala in Lhasa disguised as a stonemason. It's the truth. I froze my toes."

"And the convent?"

"Young nuns," he said mournfully. "To this day I have marks from their teeth."

Kolodny poured them more tea. Such a durable, fragile old man. Older than his seventy-four years. His coat smelled of tobacco and rain. And such a coat—a regular tent with a broken ridgepole about to collapse in a heap.

"Then how do you live?"

Serafimovich lit a fresh cigarette. "I live. But my money is gone."

"No income? No pension?"

No income, no pension. Serafimovich's explanation seemed curiously impersonal. A man who by habit scrutinizes himself with detachment. Always he had been on the move, forward, forward—the American Southwest, Siberia, New Zealand—and he had never stopped long enough to take out citizenship papers. According to his enigmatic reckoning, he was still, strictly speaking, a subject of Czar Nicholas II.

4

Kolodny was amused.

No, no. He was still under the Imperial Flag. And without American citizenship he was ineligible for the elderly indigents' pension.

"You're in bad shape," Kolodny said.

"Pretty bad." His only solace these days was the zoo. Several times a week he visited the animals. Brought them *knäckebrod* and grapes. But now, with his back against the wall, he was selling the last of his beloved technical manuals.

Flora and fauna. And when they went, there would be no more.

"What about your rent?"

"The rent is due. Overdue."

To Kolodny the solution seemed so obvious that he felt puzzled. Why hadn't the old man thought of it himself? "You must take steps. File for papers. It's the only way." Kolodny himself had been a naturalized citizen for over twenty-five years. "A simple operation: a brief interview, a few questions about the government. Very painless."

Serafimovich hitched up his eyebrows. "I am too old to learn, Alexander Alexandrovich. There are interrogations and inquisitions." The eyebrows came down. "I will die under the Imperial Flag." In his younger days his status as a citizen of the world had appealed to him. He had always equated national allegiances with cant—the last refuge of a scoundrel. "In my youth I espoused nihilism. Now I am too old. I cannot retain simple facts."

"But you remember your *Dasypus novemcinctus*."

"The *Dasypus* is different." He closed his eyes. "It is not the same thing."

"Your rent is already overdue?"

"Overdue. I told you."

"And the landlord?"

"Oriental Machiavelli." He seemed to be rocking himself very slightly. "I don't blame him. Everyone has to eat. He is threatening to change locks on the door."

"You are wasting your time at the zoo when you should be studying about the Congress."

"Perhaps."

"You have seen enough animals in your life."

"All my animals are in cages and pens nowadays." He kept rocking. "It can't be helped."

Kolodny picked up the soup bowls and brushed off the breadboard. Instead of a sink, there was only the basin in the closet. The toilet stood yellow and exposed in one corner of the small ante-room. "How much do you know about the laws of the land?"

"I know what I know, but my memory is dim."

"I have books." He scraped the bread crumbs into the toilet. "Who is Tip O'Neill?"

Serafimovich plucked the noodle from his beard and gazed at it with curiosity. "Tip O'Neill isn't important."

Kolodny seated himself on his bed. "Look here, Yuri Vassilyvich." He leaned forward and began rubbing his calves. The dampness always affected the joints, and often he kept his knees wrapped in flannel. "You are older than me, and we spring from the same soil. I'm not rich, you can see that, but I have a canvas cot and a sleeping bag packed away in the closet. When my son was a boy we went into the mountains together. Before you get your citizenship you must have instruction, and you need a small corner to sleep in. Bring your belongings. Let this room be your home. I will teach you how to pass the examination. And when you get your pension you will purchase a penthouse on Telegraph Hill."

"And live like a Turk. Give me a match, all my matches are damp." He lit his cigarette. "I am too old. I told you. Did you see the new ratel at the zoo?"

Kolodny watched Serafimovich as he packed his books back into the carton. "Think it over."

"*Mellivora capensis*," Serafimovich grunted, pushing the door open with his shoulder. "Very much like a badger," and he was gone.

5

The following day he was back, the whiskers steaming, the carton of books even soggier than before. "Machiavelli changed the lock," he belched, the cigarette still in his mouth. "Get the cot from the closet, I am bringing my things. The books are my rent, but the Smirkin seal study I keep."

He tapped the Smirkin with the handle of his cane, as if to protect it from confiscation, flicked his tobacco ashes onto the warped plywood counter, and fast-stepped out like a mechanical dwarf. Kolodny blinked at him as he padded across the street in his flapping moccasins. An electric bus was humming toward him, horn honking. Serafimovich sidestepped the bus like a bullfighter who has learned holy indifference.

6

He returned with a suitcase lashed together with twine—the handle was missing—and went back again for a laundry-type bundle wrapped in butcher paper and Scotch tape, and a five-gallon rectangular tin, dented and bent.

He began unpacking the suitcase at once. Instead of clothing, it contained documents and drawings—sketches of curious rodents and birds, topographical atlases of Africa and the Arctic marked with arrows and X's, and long yellow sheets of mathematical computations.

"Good news," he announced as he dug into a pocket for thumbtacks and proceeded to tack his pictures and maps to the walls. "They are going to construct a new pit for the apes at the zoo. About time."

Kolodny said nothing. Africa on the wall wasn't part of the bargain. But then he softened. "You'll be a good mouser," he said, unfolding the cot. The cot brought back difficult memories: his young son feeding fig bars to coons, asking questions about Cassiopeia. "The rats chew on the books. You'll be cheaper to keep than a cat. Can you cook?"

"I like rats," Serafimovich said, checking the bandage on his thumb. He wiggled the thumb. "On the seas I knew plenty of rats. I have a way with animals."

So alone, Kolodny thought. Most men live for their sons;

this one talks about rats. Like a man in a laboratory. Like a clock ticking all by itself.

7

They played chess that evening and talked about their youth. The old Russia, the land kept intact only in books. To Kolodny it was an album-world artificially tinted by his failing memory. He had left so long ago that he was unsure of his reminiscences—they were too familiar, too much like staged scenes with predictable dialogue and props. But to Serafimovich the old land was still fresh, the impressions were as varied and minute and distinct as the morning he had boarded the merchantman in Odessa. And Kolodny took note of the fact that the old man continued not only to speak but to think in his native tongue. There were roots which had never been yanked out, and this would have to be changed: the roots led to the Imperial Flag, just as his manuals kept him confined in an obsolete scientific world.

8

But the chess, at any rate, was a comfort, and Serafimovich was a crafty, a deceptively cunning opponent: it was clear that he knew, as he pored over the board, flicking ashes on the pawns, what he was about. Chess gave Kolodny a temporary reprieve from his personal griefs and regrets.

Since the death of his wife seven years ago the business had gone steadily down. He was impractical by nature, too soft to conclude the hard bargains required in the trade. Roger, his one son and early delight, had established himself in the insurance game, and by inheriting his mother's shrewd aggressiveness, had prospered. Although they lived in the same city, and Roger was apparently committed to the life of a bachelor, Kolodny never saw him. Even his name he had altered to Coleman. Well.

And the chess also helped the dealer forget the interminable winter rain and the sagging shelves of mildewing books which no one seemed to require, at least not at this time of the year.

9

Kolodny dug around among his shelves the next morning, found a manual published by the Department of Justice, a simple text in spiral-notebook form which treated in systematic fashion the basic nature and function of the federal government, and they set to work.

It gave him a quiet pleasure to observe that Serafimovich had made himself completely at home. The laundry bundle, the suitcase and the tin were shoved neatly under the cot, and the old man rocked back and forth in the Morris chair and gazed with absorption at the sketches he had tacked to the walls.

And work it was—more than the dealer had anticipated. If not a tough nut, Serafimovich was at least a slippery kernel to crack. And another thing: either the old man was hard of hearing or he chose to play deaf at convenient moments, so that much of the lecture had to be delivered at the level of a shout. *The Congress of the United States . . . the House of Representatives . . . the branches of government.* Serafimovich listened intently—but to what? Was he chewing on his mustache to indicate his understanding, or was he conducting a private dialogue involving his rare fish and fowl? *The judiciary.* It was like yanking his whiskers out, one tobacco-stained hair at a time. And each time the dealer turned the page of the manual Serafimovich's eyebrows would suffer from tortuous convolutions.

10

Kolodny gave up after an hour. "Tomorrow will be better," he suggested. "It's the first time."

Instead of replying, Serafimovich lit a cigarette, arose, browsed among the bookshelves, found an edition of John Muir's account of the Yosemite, and began reading it on the spot.

And so it went, in pretty much the same fashion, day after frustrating day. If not uncooperative, he was at least distant, aimed somehow in the wrong direction. Kolodny would lecture him, shouting instructions into his left ear, and in response he would volunteer little-known facts relative to mandrakes (*Mandragorae*) and Venus's-flytraps, lovely swamp plants which possessed leaves with double-hinged blades and an appetite for insects.

Of course Kolodny understood: his youthful commitment to nihilism had left him with an inner resistance to statutes and codes. But still. *Instead of playing ball,* he thought glumly, *we're duelling*.

Yet, paradoxically, whenever the dealer decided to call it quits, Serafimovich would wax childlike and make use of encouraging slogans. He would return stimulated from the zoo and insist that they must forge forward, they were almost on the verge, the Great Leap.

Very well. But nevertheless. Alexander Kolodny was a compassionate man, but business was truly wretched, and the winter rains didn't let up, and he was gradually losing his patience.

11

One gray afternoon, as he was attempting vainly to interrogate Serafimovich on the Bill of Rights, he noticed that the old man was even more inattentive than usual. He was staring thoughtfully at the rectangular tin under his cot. Kolodny waited. Eyes sunken, almost turned inward and aimed at the brain, Serafimovich continued his meditations. The dealer slapped the manual shut and threw it to the floor.

Serafimovich awoke, startled. "So?"

Kolodny went to the front of the store and began wiping the counter.

"Proceed," Serafimovich said, picking up the manual and brushing it off. He opened it to the section they had covered the preceding week. "Forward!"

Kolodny came back, the dustcloth still in his hand. "What's in the tin?"

"What?"

"The box under the cot—what is it?"

"Nothing." He shrugged. "Go. Look."

Kolodny threw the cloth on the table and went down on his hands and knees. Cobwebs and dust balls. Serafimovich had left tea bags all over the floor, along with his butts. Kolodny pulled the tin out. He flicked off a spider which was scuttling across his wrist. Wedging the tin between his knees, he pried off the lid.

The tin was filled with black, powdery soil, so fine that it resembled dust. Just that. He looked more closely. He reached in and felt it between his fingers. Nothing. Just dust.

He looked at the old man.

"Put it away," Serafimovich said.

"What is it?"

"It doesn't concern you. I am weary," and he arose and limped out of the room.

12

But during supper that night, after describing in great detail the progress that had been made on the pit for the apes, he changed his mind and asked the bookdealer to drag out the tin again.

Kolodny dragged out the tin. He pried off the lid.

"In this tin," Serafimovich said gravely, as though delivering his own funeral oration, "is our mother soil. This is our soil. You understand what I say, Alexander Alexandrovich. This soil I dug up from a frozen field near Murmansk when I was a young man. A young man. I have kept it, my friend, because this has been country and home. This soil. The soil from which our seed sprang."

He took the tin, balanced it on his lap, and inhaled the dust, as though human bones lay buried in it—bones of Father and

Mamushka and girls he had loved. Bones of uncles in fur coats and comrades in school.

"I had been sailing, you know. On the *Catherine the Great*—what a name for a freighter! One day we docked in Murmansk. High noon. Early spring. I stood on the wharf. I looked at the sledges and the horses, steaming, and the dockhands stamping their boots in the snow. Soon we would be off again, Portugal, Argentina. How long would we be gone? No one knew. We went where the cargo was—if in hell, then to hell. And with the sun, and the snow, and the horses, I felt a desire to bring back to my cabin some part of the land where my seed was begun."

He rocked back and forth. "I started to walk through the snow. It was like broken glass, the snow. Dear God, the cold! I searched for a field. From a tailor's wife whose husband had recently perished I bought the tin—she had used it for tea—and borrowed a shovel. I never saw such a blunt shovel. And I began to dig. As I dug, the tailor's wife told me a long tale about how her husband had died. Some kind of disease of the blood. I kept digging. *God sees everything!* she wept, and I cried *Amen!* and kept digging. I had to dig deep before I found blackness. It was frozen, the earth, like a great shelf of stone, but finally I had hacked out several chunks. I hacked until I had enough for this tin."

He let the tin slide between his legs to the floor. "You understand me, Alexander Alexandrovich. From that day it has been with me, this dust. I carried it with me through four continents. A fact. Sometimes on my mule, sometimes strapped to my back. Poor old Pedro."

He exhaled. Where was that breath coming from?

"On certain afternoons, when I am tired and my memory is sharp, full of visions and smells of the past, I take off the cover and savor this soil, and I hold it against my stomach and ribs. Against my bowels. This is my home, after all. My nose understands this rare smell," and he frowned a fierce frown:

for a moment the old man turned gargoyle. Then his face relaxed. "And the animals know."

"The animals know?"

"I communicate with them."

Kolodny bent over the tin. It smelled more like dust from an attic than earth from a cold Russian field, and there was also something of the sea in it, a faint trace of canvas and hemp.

Bad business, bad business. Obviously this was part of his problem. Too many knots tying him to the past. Dust and wild animals. It was surely bad business. He was clearly not ready to surrender the tin.

13

Of course they weren't prepared—preparation for him meant tin-sniffing and spinning his yarns—but Kolodny had submitted all the documents and forms, along with a passport-type photo he had paid for himself (a deplorable shot, like a circus portrait of The World's Oldest Living Homo Sapiens), and the day of the examination came. They took the bus to the federal building on Sansome Street. Although they were late, Serafimovich seemed unbearably calm. Optimistic. "The Potala," he winked as they walked through the lobby.

The examiner's name was T. J. Hunter and his head was a neatly combed circle—a friction-free head which the Lord had designed for utility. Kolodny disliked him at once. He reminded him of Roger and his insurance policies. Clinical.

Serafimovich seated himself at the side of the desk and Kolodny took a chair against the beaver-board partition, under a photograph of the Justices of the Supreme Court.

"Back," Hunter droned, waving his ball-point pen at Kolodny. "Can't have you here. Back to the waiting room." A ventriloquist: his lips didn't move but the words came out anyway. He kept his tongue rolled up in the back of his nose. Serafimovich folded his hands. His beard quivered.

"The old man has bad ears," Kolodny said.

The examiner leaned back in his swivel chair, thoughtful and annoyed. His head was like a balloon with a pinprick. The gas was leaking out slowly.

"His hearing is bad," Kolodny insisted.

"Hard of hearing, are you?" Hunter asked.

Serafimovich crossed his legs and scowled at the bookdealer. "No."

14

It was too hot in the waiting room. Too many pregnant women, too many clerks wielding rubber stamps. The man sitting half-asleep in the back row looked too much like a CIA agent. Kolodny roamed through the halls with his hands in his pockets, read the bulletin boards, filled his mouth with warm water from the fountain, studied the faces of the clerks and the elevator operators, and stared out the window at San Francisco Bay, gray and rainswept below him. Over there, out of view behind the hill, was Clement Street and the shop. Today, perhaps, customers were waiting for him.

Not likely. Mount Tamalpais to the north rose up pale and unlovely, its haunches immersed in a mist which washed out depth and shade and left everything underexposed. He saw the ridge where he used to go hiking with Roger. His breath was steaming up the glass. He wiped it off.

And almost directly below him, slightly to the left, the financial district and the fancy aluminum building where Roger sat with his pushbutton phones.

Kolodny forced his eyes back to the mountain. There is also destruction in distance: either end of the telescope bruises and robs.

15

Then he heard Hunter's voice summoning him from the end of the hall. "Come in here," he demanded, his tongue in his nose. "I can't spend the whole morning on one deaf old man."

Kolodny went into the office and sat down.

"Hallo," Serafimovich said brightly, uncrossing his legs. "I am finished?"

Hunter didn't even look at him. He rubbed his eyes. "How many states in the Union?"

"Alabama —"

"How many houses in Congress?"

Serafimovich opened his mouth, then closed it. He looked at Kolodny. The bookdealer remained deadpan.

Hunter droned on. "How many branches in the government? What are the branches?"

"In the government," Kolodny shouted, mouthing his words into the old man's left ear, "how many *branches?*"

"High Court—"

Hunter waited, one shoe under the other.

"Legislature—senators." Pause. "Senators."

Hunter reversed his feet. "Checks and balances—what does that mean?"

"Checks and balances," Kolodny said.

"Checks and balances," Hunter repeated.

The beard quivered.

Hunter flipped the page of the examination booklet. "How many years does a President serve?"

Serafimovich sat up, then leaned forward. "Which one?"

Silence.

"What should I do with this old man?" Hunter asked. "He doesn't know what I'm talking about."

Serafimovich cleared his throat. "You permit me to smoke, brother?"

"Smoke," Hunter said. "You don't need my permission to smoke."

They looked at each other. Serafimovich blew smoke through his nose.

"He's pretty old," Kolodny suggested.

16

As they stepped into the elevator Serafimovich fluffed out his whiskers. "Okay?"

Kolodny stared blankly at the emergency-exit instructions. "Fine."

"I passed?"

"No."

The eyebrows went to work.

"Button your coat. It's still raining."

"I am tired," he said. "I—," and he rapped his cane against the elevator wall. Down plunged the steel box, beneath streets and houses, and lower and lower. "We will try again," Serafimovich said, and the steel cage went deeper and yet farther down.

17

So they picked up the pieces. Kolodny put the old man on a rigid schedule: when to eat, when to study, when to pay court to tigers and apes. He employed sundry threats. He resorted to bribery: promises of all the *pelmeni* he could eat. Serafimovich looked grave, twisted his beard between his fingers and responded as one might have expected. Kolodny brought up the geographical locations of the prairie states and Serafimovich plunged into a sermon on partridges. Gallinaceous fowl. "A *Perdix perdix* of the subspecies *Perdicinae*—a gray partridge I had painstakingly trained—and I would call to him, as though he were a regular seafowl: Hulloa there, Mishka, you foolish *Perdix,* how's the weather upstairs?"

"You will not get your papers," Kolodny assured him. "You will die under the Imperial Flag."

". . . and a frigate bird who had followed our ship out of Newfoundland, a *Fregata aquila* . . . ."

And suddenly Kolodny felt the burden of his years on his shoulders and back. For one stone-cold moment he felt the death of his wife and the indifference of his son, and the rain kept on falling, and the business was going kaput.

He struggled to put on his raincoat. "Enough!" One sleeve had been pulled inside out. "I'm going for air. Watch the store."

Serafimovich glanced up. "What's the matter?"

"I don't know."

"Men must focus their eyes on essentials."

18

Kolodny regretted his temper at once, before he had reached Ninth Avenue. Had he offended the old man? Would he pack up and leave? But where would he go? Already he saw Serafimovich removing his maps from the walls, slipping the tacks into his pocket, packing his suitcase, wiping the cobwebs from the tin. He hurried back to the shop.

Dear God, he had done it. The shade was down and the CLOSED sign lay propped on the sill. Kolodny stared at the sign. He was cursed—a man destined to suffer a series of losses. Even the key was rebelling: it stuck in the lock.

19

But there he was, the old reprobate, lying on his cot, a book propped against his knees. Kolodny said nothing. He felt greatly relieved. What are manuals and flags? Serafimovich could stay with him, eat his soup *ad infinitum.* He wanted him to stay. And he made a decision: there would be no more lessons or interrogations.

"Still raining," Serafimovich observed, noting the puddle Kolodny was leaving on the floor.

"Still raining." He shook out his raincoat. "Let's have tea."

20

And the following day, as if in reaction to the bookdealer's new policy, the inexplicable card came. How to account for it? An administrative error? A clerical mistake?

It was no mistake. An official postcard, Department of

Immigration and Naturalization, signed T.J.H. Kolodny was dumbfounded. He had misjudged this man Hunter. Hunter had bowels, after all, and a heart.

The card advised that Yuri V. Serafimovich had successfully passed the naturalization examination and would be sworn in at the Federal Courthouse on the twenty-first of the month, at 3 P.M., Judge Harry Neumann presiding.

21

On the day of the swearing in Kolodny arranged to close the shop early and meet Serafimovich at the New Manchuria for dinner. There are things men must celebrate. Already he had bought him a full pound of halvah—Serafimovich was childishly fond of halvah—and a carton of Camels. "First an early dinner," the bookdealer said, "then we'll go to the zoo. Since my boy graduated from high school I haven't been to the zoo."

"Good!" Serafimovich broke off a large chunk of halvah, leaving crumbs on his coat and the floor. He began shoving it into his beard. "I want to take a few notes. I told you about the new ratel, the rare *Mellivora capensis*—."

"For God's sake, don't plunge into lectures on ratels! You'll be late for the swearing in. The New Manchuria—you know where it is? Brush your coat."

"I know where it is, but we'll have to eat fast. They lock the zoo gates at five."

"Wait a minute. Five. No. Better first go to the zoo. Then we can take the whole night with our meal, and I'll order a bottle of kvass."

"I'm going," Serafimovich said. "The zoo first. I'll be there before you. Look for me. I'll be smoking your Camels in front of the ratel."

22

A customer came in looking for Lazhechnikov's *House of Ice*. Kolodny knew he had it, but it was difficult to find. By the time he had ferreted out the volume, Serafimovich had departed, and Kolodny noticed that he had taken the tin with him. Incorrigible! Crumbs of halvah and a tin in a dignified courthouse!

23

Business was unaccountably brisk that afternoon, a group of language students from Berkeley, a good omen, but it meant that Kolodny was delayed.

Finally he was able to close up the shop. He took the streetcar to the zoo. Almost closing time, and the rain had given way to a dense fog which was blowing in from the ocean in large pockets, like great, heavy opera-house curtains.

Serafimovich wasn't at the ratel's cage, or anywhere else. Over the loudspeaker a voice announced that the zoo was closing. Where was he? Avoiding the watchmen and caretakers, who were whirring about in the fog on three-wheeled scooters, he slipped past the various animal shelters. He gave silent thanks for the fog and the poor visibility.

Yuri Vassilyvich. The fog kept rearranging itself around him. Kolodny tiptoed on, soles squeaking, past the oxen and ibex, the apes and the pronghorn, and then he discovered the old man.

Serafimovich was shuffling from compound to compound, from railing to railing, and each time he stopped he plunged his hand into the tin box and scattered the dust among the beasts. Kolodny kept his distance and peered through the curtains of fog. When Serafimovich stopped, Kolodny stopped. When he moved, the bookdealer went forward. Dust to the elephants, dust to the imprisoned cats. Like a planter the old man was sowing his dust.

The Blum Invitation

1

"The glissando," Blum said at the conclusion of the second act. "A glissando for a miracle," and he pulled out his handkerchief.

Andrew Pelzner looked at him.

"The harp glissando." His forefinger went *whoosh*. "The flight of the spear."

Pelzner reexamined the program notes as Blum pushed up his glasses and wiped his eyes. The Festspielhaus lights came on slowly, unevenly, like paint flowing down a primed canvas. Blum reached for his cigarettes. Pelzner pushed himself out of his seat and Blum followed him outside, an unlit cigarette between his fingers. This was how they met.

Outside Blum talked energetically about the production. Even in the best houses abroad, he said, lipping his cigarette without inhaling, Wagner isn't quite right. It is not the same thing. Authenticity is important—the strings need German air. Send the whole orchestra to New York: you will not have a proper glissando.

Pelzner made no reply and attempted to shake off the stout little man. In vain.

After the *Parsifal* Blum accompanied Pelzner to the Rienzi Bar and insisted on paying for his drink. The little man was Corsican, and he had a habit of standing on tiptoe and picking at his nails behind his back as he talked. Perhaps it aided his thinking. His mustache was a postage stamp quickly slapped on at an angle.

"The Amfortas sang through his ears," Blum observed, sounding like a physician.

Pelzner nodded. Again the headache.

"Through his ears." The Corsican took off his glasses and blinked at the young man's reflection in the mirror. "You are not with the Kaiser Aluminum crowd?"

"No."

Blum replaced his spectacles.

2

The crowd filtered out, but the two men remained in the bar and Blum talked about *Parsifal*. "I am always a little surprised," he said, eyeing the cubes in his glass as though his innermost thoughts lay there, frozen fast in the ice, "I'm surprised to discover how moved I become when the spear heals the wound of the king." Pulling out the wrinkled handkerchief, he blew his nose, then wiped his forehead. "Myself, I have no talent. None. But I am a man of feeling."

Pelzner picked up his coat and slipped out of the bar while the Corsican was in the men's room. He began walking briskly up the hill to the hotel, his headache sliding over his eyes like a visor, his open coat flapping. A clear night: cardboard trees. The moon had settled itself neatly on top of the Festspielhaus, and his shadow preceded him, stretching and shrinking like rubber.

The beams of a car cut his shadow in two. "Lift?" The Corsican had stuck his head out of the cab.

Pelzner buttoned his coat. "I'm walking."

"I will join you!" And Blum bounded out.

As they walked up the hill Blum kept taking deep breaths. He crossed his hands over his chest. Bayreuth, Bayreuth. And Pelzner agreed: there was something rare here.

"But perhaps it is all stage machinery," Blum said.

Pelzner stopped. A coat button had come off. He bent down and slipped it into his pocket.

They had a final drink in the hotel bar, and, before retiring, Blum—apparently from habit—prepared to jot down the young American's name in his notebook. Pelzner looked at the oversized address pad crammed with business cards, clippings and notes. Blum kept it intact with the help of a black elastic band, like a garter.

Blum wrote out the name and then stared at it, puzzled, his mustache off-center, as though he couldn't quite decipher his own hasty scrawl. Pelzner made his face wooden. He knew what it was.

"But I read your book!" Blum said, still slightly uncertain. He leaned forward for a better look.

3

Pelzner sat on the bed in his room and examined his coat. Another button was loose. When one button gets loose all the buttons get loose. And now the book again. It was odd, unexpected, this business with Blum, like the pain in a molar just recently filled. Pelzner threw the coat over a chair and felt around for the book with the tips of his fingers. He could almost feel it wedged in his skull: a coarse iron object, overturned and beginning to rust. It had given him a few pleasant moments but had finally taken on a wrong kind of weight and exhausted him, shamed him away from Chicago. And now it continued to drain him, each time he was caught unawares and confronted with it.

He reached for the coat, pulled off the second button, and turned it around in his hand like a coin.

4

The next morning Blum intercepted him in the lobby, and Pelzner felt the familiar frustration with himself, with his passive inability to slam doors and perform abrupt exits. Of course Blum also noticed the young man's mild nature, and this intrigued him. So unlike Pelzner's big brawling novel, a barbaric performance with muscle and bone.

The little man insisted on lunch, and after lunch they drove through the countryside in a rented Opel. Blum was attending a convention of hotel owners, but that was only an excuse. "I come here for Bayreuth," he said, pointing his finger at his heart. His wife had remained in Corsica, not far from Palmetto, where they owned a resort and some olive orchards. His only son Gerard had been killed in the Algerian war. "You have similar eyes," Blum said, grasping the wheel with both hands, "very dark," and he honked the horn sadly.

Pelzner glanced out the window. The sun seemed to be aiming its light at a church in the distance. The steeple shot off little sparks.

Blum started discussing the book. "Lots of motion. Nothing lying around for the reader to kick into life. I was very impressed."

"It wasn't exactly a roaring success," Pelzner said, rolling down the window and smelling the fields. He wiped his hand on his knee: the handle felt tacky. "How did you find it?"

"I have a man in Munich."

They drove for a while in silence, and then Blum said, "I know how you feel. You are despondent. Flop book. Who wouldn't? Every page dipped in blood. And that's how it is." He shifted to third. "I can admire—all the howling and hopping is left for your kind."

"I don't think I am hopping," Pelzner said.

5

Two days went by and Pelzner saw no more of him. Then the Corsican popped up again, next to him in the Festspielhaus, with the announcement: "I have carefully gone over your book. My reaction was right."

Pelzner folded his program and put it away. This peculiar man.

"It has a face," Blum insisted. "It has facial expressions. There is more than black on white. This means something."

"You're a generous man," Pelzner said.

Blum peered at him, as though he were sighting him through a periscope. The lights in the theater were dimming, the shadows lengthening, spiraling up to the ceiling. Blum edged closer. "You're not working. Correct?"

Pelzner joined in the applause for the conductor.

"Listen, my friend," Blum whispered. He brought his hands together in an attitude of prayer. "I love art but I have no talent. In me there is no talent."

The overture.

Blum edged closer. "Look at me now. I am not a King Midas, but I'm not wearing rags. My hotel brings me small security. Corsica is peculiar—more people depart than arrive. Depopulation. Houses are easily available, and the food is cheap. The tourists admire it because it is not quite civilized. The young people flee for the same reason. Near my hotel I have some old houses. Empty houses. Stone. During the time of harvest I hire people to pick the olives, but the houses are empty. Come to Palmetto and look at my houses. They are near the hotel, but not too near. They are in the hills, above the terraces, a half hour from the village. By horse only ten minutes. I have horses. In Corsica you will write something good. Silence you will have. Above all, what you have in your book—this living face—you will continue. Continue this face."

Pelzner cleared his throat.

"You have no money," Blum said. "Correct?"

Pelzner stared at the stage. The divorce and the flight from Chicago had been expensive.

"Food is cheap." The curtain was going up. "There will be no rent. You can stay for a few weeks, a few months, and then leave. No obligations. I am only a hotel man, a gnat, but I love art. I see art in your hands and your eyes. Your skin has a poor color."

Pelzner glared at Blum fiercely. The opera had begun. Blum was not intimidated.

"In the morning I will write to my wife. A remarkable woman. You can come down whenever you wish, and then leave when it is time to leave. No one will disturb you—you need solitude to create. You have a typewriter?"

"I don't need a typewriter."

"I will lend you a large office typewriter. Olympia. There is little furniture in the houses, and the windows have no glass. No ornamentation, no fancy contrivances. Your book will be so. Genuine."

"I've already made plans," Pelzner lied. "I am visiting a friend in Amsterdam."

"I leave on Friday," Blum whispered. "First Munich, then Marseilles. We will go down together."

6

The Hotel Corse was surrounded by irregular terraces on all sides, each circle slightly lighter in coloring than the one beneath it. The bottom of the empty swimming pool was crisscrossed with bicycle tracks, and behind the pool there were two tennis courts at right angles to each other with poorly mended nets.

Pelzner stepped from the lobby into the dining salon. A local girl with a surly expression was setting silver for the noon meal. Next to the French doors was a platform for a dance band. Except for the clinking of the silver and the sound of a bird squawking somewhere in the distance, the place was silent. Blum had driven his wife to Ajaccio for a dental appointment.

Pelzner opened the French doors and stepped into the Corsican sun. A short distance to the left, on the widest terrace, were the riding stables. Although the hotel was of medium size, there were only six registered guests. More would come later in the season.

Blum hadn't deceived him: the island was lovely. Pelzner went to look at the horses. The horses were not much to look at—listless and overfed. He climbed higher, up to the second terrace, then to the third, and soon found himself on the road leading to Palmetto.

7

In the center of Palmetto was a square with a fountain

which gave little water. Pelzner sat on a circular stone bench and squinted at the houses. Everything glared, everything was white, everything dazzled. There was not one sun, but several, in various parts of the square, arranged like klieg lights. He shielded his eyes from the glare. Flatness, flatness, no depth, no shadows. The houses had been painted in without outlines.

When the Ajaccio bus rolled into the square with its exhaust banging, Pelzner hesitated, looked at the driver, who seemed to be waiting for him, and climbed aboard. As he rode to Ajaccio he looked at the bleached countryside. Behind them, inhaling the dust of the bus like an escort, was a heavy-set man on a motorcycle. They descended and passed through a fishing village that was also filled with suns, but the houses and nets were the color of mustard.

He found Ajaccio larger than he'd expected, a city of over 40,000 souls. There were memorials to Bonaparte. He went roaming up and down the streets in hopes of spotting Blum's Fiat, but he couldn't locate it. He walked about aimlessly.

When he reboarded the Palmetto bus, the engine made a great racket, like Sten guns announcing an ambush. He sat next to one of the Americans from the Hotel Corse, a middle-aged man with hair that came down to his shoulders and an amulet around his neck. The man taught civics and woodworking in a junior high school in Toledo. He talked a great deal, mostly about the Corsican girls, the young ones, whose flesh, he said, playing with the rings on his fingers, was like flesh of fried capon.

8

Pelzner's stone house was surrounded by a wall which had a wooden gate and a padlock. The people of Palmetto, Blum said, were no better than thieves. If he didn't keep the orchard locked, the olives disappeared from the trees. The front of the house faced an untended vegetable garden. The back rested almost on the edge of a cliff that rose up from the bay. At the bottom was a crescent-shaped beach, but the descent looked hazardous.

As Blum had warned, the windows had no glass, only wooden shutters. They seemed better without glass. At night the green shutters were filled with noises, and at sunrise the sea was yellow and the Corsican hills hurled themselves lengthwise against the yellowish sky.

Pelzner was left to himself for a few days. A man from the hotel brought his food on a donkey. "From the boss," he would say, handing him the wicker basket, and he'd ride away kicking the ribs of the donkey.

Then Blum came riding in through the open gate one morning, and he was leading a second horse behind him.

"I was told," Blum grunted, adjusting Pelzner's stirrup, "that already you've been to Ajaccio."

"I took the bus in the day you went to the dentist."

"Whenever you feel like going in, I can lend you a car. It's a 1953 car, but it's a car."

"The bus is all right, but they need a new motor."

"They need a new bus." He pushed his riding crop into his belt. "You met one of my guests on the bus."

"A schoolteacher from Ohio."

"An unusual man—he has studied the occult. I mentioned to him that you write."

Pelzner nodded and looked at the ears of his horse. The ears were turned back.

Blum flicked his rein. His horse had been going around in a circle. "You were looking for pleasure in Ajaccio?"

Pelzner gave him a blank look.

"Very well," Blum said, resting his hand on the pommel.

9

Pelzner usually slept late and attempted to write in the afternoons. He began taking notes. No plot, yet—just characters in outline and splinters of dialogue. His father, a Maxwell Street clothing merchant, was there, and Pelzner was trying to put it down straight. He had trouble describing his wife because she kept changing herself in his head. When the sun began to set and the shadows slid out of their crevices, he went to the hotel for supper and companionship. Although jealous of his privacy, he was almost constantly lonely. Several times he ran into the Toledo teacher, a bachelor, and got regularly beaten at tennis. They played in the evenings and he had difficulty keeping track of the ball, which dissolved in the dark, then reappeared out of nowhere. Through the teacher he was introduced to the other guests.

On the nights that dances were scheduled for the Hotel Corse Pelzner went to the village to sample the wines and study the local inhabitants. Blum disliked them, they were slothful and arrogant and had Communist leanings. Italian blood. And because Pelzner kept to himself and rarely spoke to anyone, and because he was looked upon as a member of the Blum menagerie, he was received by the people of Palmetto with coolness. The heavy man with the motorcycle owned the village tavern and made disparaging remarks about him, the indolent American scribbler, in the local dialect. His daughter was a maid at the Hotel Corse, and for this the fat man nursed a grudge against all tourists, especially American, who treated his girl, so he claimed, like a common Sicilian.

10

Madame Blum was enigmatic but kind. She had read the book. A handsome woman, she was thirteen years younger than her husband and played an intense game of tennis. She enjoyed talking opera and art, but whenever Blum came upon the scene she withdrew. She gave Pelzner the freedom of the library, which was closed to the regular guests except on special request. Here he could browse through their books and listen to Blum's operatic recordings.

"One of his passions," Madame Blum said, lifting the dust cover of the impressive sound system. "Every year to

Bayreuth, to Milan. He knows many singers. He has aided several. An atonement, he says, for his own lack of talent. He corresponds with top names."

"With top names?"

She laughed. "With the people at the top."

He spent many evenings listening to the Blum recordings. Sometimes he would pull out a number of records and mix them up and let one follow the other, with the sequence intentionally destroyed. Then he'd half-listen to the voices as he blocked out the next chapter of the book, and when Madame Blum entered the library in her swishy tennis outfit he'd ask, "What is this?" and she'd reply, "This is *Lulu,*" or "This is *Suor Angelica,*" or "This is *Adriana Lecouvreur,*" and she'd generally conclude with the phrase, "One of his favorites."

One morning, when Blum was away in Ajaccio ordering new lawn umbrellas and chairs, she came on foot to the stone house, stayed a couple of hours, and left Pelzner worn out and confused. If Bernard knew, she said calmly, brushing his hair with her hand, they'd behold an unspeakable scene.

In the library that evening, as Pelzner took her hand and held it against his cheek, she arose and said matter-of-factly, "There will be no more," and there wasn't.

11

Pelzner was gradually forgetting that first novel. He'd been hungry for motion and blood, but his hungers had made him impatient. The book had turned into a gimmick he'd learned to manipulate, a catalogue of outrageous adventures, sacred madness and inspirational sex. The tunes had been easy to learn, and he'd blown like a wild man. But in time he discovered that all the breathless depictions of the author as free spirit were an innocent shuck, like the dull, garbled Wisdom of the East which he thought would add weight to the horny escapades. Too late. When he returned to Chicago from the West Coast he discovered that the big shuck had beaten him home. People were looking at him through the lens of the book. Some were believing his words; others saw what he actually was.

He had misrepresented himself.

12

But then the peculiar thing happened. Three of the guests at the Hotel Corse approached him one evening after tennis with copies of his novel in their hands. They requested his autograph—and, if it wouldn't be too much trouble, a brief personal greeting. "Something to bring home to Toledo," the schoolteacher said, fingering the amulet on his chest.

Blum was responsible, of course. Characteristic. He had ordered a dozen copies from his man in Munich. Directly and indirectly, in various ways, the hotel man had been spreading the word about his new protegé. As a climax to his proselytizing, he had left a gift-wrapped copy of the book in each of the occupied rooms, on the bureau, with a card: *Compliments Bernard Blum*. Pelzner thanked him and spent less and less time at the hotel. But then there was the business of the bazaar.

13

One of the maids at the hotel—the daughter of the obese innkeeper—had helped herself to one of the unclaimed copies of the book. She could read no English, but took it home without removing the wrapping as a convenient offering for the annual Peter and Paul bazaar. The bazaar was held in the square. The tables radiated like spokes from the circular fountain and the priest supervised the activities.

Father Alembert had taught himself English during the war. He roamed from table to table, his hands constantly in motion, his steel-rimmed spectacles grimy with dust. Almost by accident he spotted the book and removed the gift-wrapping. He stared at the cover: a pop art nude straddling a flame-colored Kawasaki.

After skimming through a few pages in the privacy of his

study, he confiscated the volume and rebuked the girl for her carelessness, not because she had committed a sin but because he had been aroused by the book's lurid passages. A susceptible man.

Soon the villagers were pointing to Pelzner as a manufacturer of pornography. Now the corpulent innkeeper had an even better reason for disliking this taciturn young man from Chicago: he had brought his daughter into disfavor with Father Alembert, and that on the eve of her engagement to a young man who boasted his own pilot's license.

14

In the afternoons, as he wrote, Pelzner found himself tiring easily, and too soon, and it was clear that the pattern was being repeated. He was losing control of the new manuscript. Page after page, there was something incorrect, like a smudge that you cannot erase. Already the man he had tried to depict as his father had turned into Zorba the Greek.

Whenever the supply of writing materials ran low, Blum rode up on his gelding, like a clairvoyant, with a packet of paper and a fresh ribbon for the Olympia. Pelzner never bothered with the ribbons. By now he had several reels on the shelf. Blum would also bring wine and fresh fruit. Sometimes a cheese. Before leaving, he'd glance at the manuscript and grunt to himself. Like a farmer in his fields.

15

Some days, when Pelzner didn't feel like writing at all, the two of them would sit on stiff wooden chairs in the middle of the vegetable garden and talk. Blum was fond of quotations: "Balzac says that incessant labor is as much the law of art as it is of life." On one occasion, a very hot day, he suggested a swim, but the day was too hot and the path much too steep. When Pelzner mentioned the Peter and Paul bazaar, Blum spat on the weeds.

He went into the house as though he were living in it. Flicking his crop like a flyswatter, he held his breath, then said, "Try this wine. From the grapes north of Bastia."

As they sampled the wine, Blum unbuttoned his jacket—he'd been eating too much—and picked up the top page of the manuscript. He read it half-aloud, stumbling slightly over some of the words. He went on to the next page. "How's the wine?"

Pelzner took the crop from the table, tested its balance and weight, looked at Blum in his half-buttoned jacket and boots, and proceeded to bend it. The crop bent, but it would not snap. He set it down. Blum read two more pages and laid the manuscript aside. Up he went, on his toes. "Good." The mustache was off-center. "Good good."

"Yes?"

"The face is still there."

16

Pelzner wrote no more that day, nor the next. Instead, he climbed down the cliff to the beach and stretched out on the sand. He dug his hands into the sand. The loss of control was an actual feeling. Grainy. He could feel it caught under his fingernails. He jumped up, saw his shadow slide over the sand, and began hopping around on one foot.

He climbed up to the stone house, washed his face under the pump, changed his shirt, and went to the village.

Bossa Nova and Beatles: a loudspeaker had been strapped to the fountain and the phonograph was going full blast. The obese innkeeper was throwing an engagement party for his daughter, who had finally hooked the young man with the pilot's license.

Pelzner entered the inn. A small girl balancing a tray on one shoulder offered him a tumbler of wine. He took it and seated himself at one of the corner tables. The villagers were dancing. He watched the older men and women as they danced. He watched their expressions.

He sat there for a long time and observed them. The same dozen discs were replayed over and over again. When he arose to leave, the floor seemed to be curving away from his feet. He'd been funnelling the wine in, steadily and mechanically, without thinking about it. He lowered himself carefully into his chair. The innkeeper's daughter went into the kitchen, her new hairdo about to get snagged on the beams. In the long yellow mirror he could see the older men and women solemnly Foxtrotting to the Beatles. The frame of the mirror was ornamented with cherubs of gold, all registering beatific visions. He could see just the top of his head and his eyes reflected in the glass.

17

He accepted yet another tumbler of wine, and when he looked into the mirror again he noticed that the corpulent innkeeper was observing him sadly from a corner of the room. The innkeeper's head seemed unbearably heavy. The masses of flesh, slabs of olive and gray, contrasted with his steady and sorrowful eyes. Pelzner's left knee began trembling. He steadied it with his hand. The girl came out of the kitchen, stared boldly at Pelzner, and busied herself behind the bar with a cold look of distaste. The cash register on top of the bar was a rococo piece of machinery. Again Pelzner glanced into the mirror.

Yes. The innkeeper was gazing upon him with sadness and something like pain.

18

Pelzner slid down the terraces without bothering to follow the path. He circled around the hotel, gagged into the dark empty pool, and went to the stone house.

There was a big moon that night, and it kept getting bigger, so that eventually it would fill up the entire sky. Pelzner fell asleep in the middle of the vegetable garden, on the two chairs, with his arm covering his eyes.

19

When he awoke he saw that it would be a hot day. He went into the stone house. He packed his belongings, tied up the manuscript and knotted the twine with a number of permanent knots. He took his coat from the hanger. Another button was about to come off. He removed it and added it to his collection.

At the inn, the engaged girl, looking bleary and disheveled, was taking down the drapes from the windows. They were coated with cobwebs. Pelzner slipped the manuscript under the rococo cash register and whistled to her, as though he were calling a dog.

20

That morning the village was drowning in white, and the suns were all around him, getting in his way. But it was a different time of the year, and now, in addition to the suns, there were shadows making huge geometrical thrusts at the white. He sat on the circular stone bench, his suitcase between his knees, and looked at the fountain. He watched the slow, silent dripping of the water. The black-frocked priest crossed the square with quick, delicate steps, and following him was a cat with a body which seemed hollow, sucked empty of flesh. Neither of them made a sound.

Pelzner could hear his own breathing deep inside his ears. He rested his back against the dazzling white fountain and looked through the slits of his eyes at the shadow he threw. The air was filled with dead fish. His shoelace was untied.

As he bent over to tie his shoelace the square began exploding and dust whirled around him. The Ajaccio bus circled around the fountain and squealed to a halt in front of the inn. The old bus was running on five cylinders and there was a constant backfiring from the exhaust.

Pelzner sat in the last row, next to a man holding a wire cage with a chicken. The bus exploded all the way into Ajaccio.

Mutability and the Meat Loaf

1

The hammock was a comfort. Khoslov swung back and forth with the cat in his arms, his eyes following the sweep of the leaves as they tilted and righted themselves. The canvas beneath him felt rigid and lashed to the lawn: it was the sky which was swinging, a darkening heaven of peaches and bunches of leaves, back and forth, now and then snapping slightly, then gliding away. As he swung he kept glancing at the various sections of the garden—the shrubs and the ferns, the flagstones, the stakes which the dogs had knocked loose. Recently it had somehow gone out of control, fallen prey to all manner of pests, fungi, accidents, weeds. He scratched the swiveling ears of the cat, an old tom with a face like an owl. Very soon Nikolai would be home and they'd have a good dinner of meat loaf and bread, all of them, the whole tribe.

He could feel the rough tongue of the cat on his wrist. Figaro was licking the strap of his watch. As Khoslov checked his watch he felt suddenly dizzy. The luminous dial sliced into the sky and swung up.

2

Must be finished. He could smell it already, the juice of the beef, mixed with onions and dill weed, in the middle of the garden, intermingling with the fragrance of roses and licorice and plums hanging down from the trees. His eyes followed the curves of the paths as they circled and crossed like a loose, lovely knot. He had neglected this place. The grandifloras were wilted, the hybrid teas were unpruned. Her illness had taken up most of his energy and time. The roses might turn into a fiasco.

Well. He unhooked Figaro from his vest. The cat was discarding his fur. Khoslov ran his hand down his black, wrinkled vest. For years you don't wear things like vests, and then suddenly here are the vests. Fashions change, cats and flowers keep their style. He buried his nose in the fur. Figaro would be twelve in October. Go, discard—what is hair?

3

Alberto and Buster crouched under the hammock and blinked solemnly in the direction of the kitchen. They kept their tails tight against their ribs.

Enough. Khoslov eased the cat off, struggled out of the hammock, the front of his coat full of hair, and went into the kitchen to look at the meat loaf. He left the kitchen door open. The single deep line in his forehead, and the incisions of age, like the cuts from a knife, gave his face the appearance of tin plate. His features were sections of metal, some soldered together, some joined at the corners with hinges. The whippets followed him in uncertainly, tails slapping against the cupboards and walls. This was still new to them. They sniffed the seats of the chairs and glanced discreetly down the dark hall, ready to beat a judicious retreat. The evening breeze blowing down from the low coastal range spiraled through the dark house, in one window and out another; it riffled the paper napkins on the table, shook the plastic dwarf phlox on the Formica counter.

4

The counter was a mess—cigarette butts, a number of empty Schweppes bottles, a half-eaten cake in a squashed bakery box. Khoslov opened the oven door and pulled out the tray with a hot pad shaped like a huge mitten. His hinges moved slightly, leaving him suddenly with no expression at all. He whistled. The meat was still gray. He turned the dial up to 400, pushed Alberto away from the roasting pan, and slid the loaf back inside.

Buster scratched himself fiercely. He lunged backward

and sank his teeth into the folds of his neck, below the brass-studded collar. They were being devoured by the fleas, both of them. Khoslov threw the big mitten on the counter and studied the sink like a sculptor assessing his work. The sink was filled with grease-covered dishes and pans, eggshells, half-consumed baked potatoes, brown mugs, Anna's blue rubber gloves—all of it somehow coming together and forming a construct of complementary shapes. Figaro padded into the kitchen and froze, one paw up, his eyes watching a moth which kept striking itself against the overhead light. The dogs whined.

5

"Keep your shirt on," Khoslov said to the pups. "He'll be home in a minute or two," and he went with them out to the garden again. For the first time he noticed the fence. It was leaning over into Schwann's yard, just in back of the dog house. The dog house was a beautiful kennel, bright red, made to look like a barn, with a real weathervane. So the fence posts are starting to rot. He whistled. The wrong things are rotting out here, and the wrong things are starting to grow. He lay down in the hammock.

Scene by scene, blur by blur, one improperly focused impression at a time, he backtracked. He tried to put into some kind of meaningful order the series of jumbled events leading back to the moment when she had turned from the can opener attached to the wall, her mouth gaping in what seemed to be a long yawn, her hands plucking at her apron. She had fallen to the floor like an overturned flask, with a rattle of glasses and bone. Long after they had taken her away in the ambulance, the pups barking their heads off, the can of ravioli remained stuck in the wall opener. Her glasses, he guessed, were still gathering dust under the refrigerator.

6

He looked at his wristwatch again. The skin on the knuckle of his forefinger was scraped, partly off. Where had he scraped it? He chewed on the loose flap of skin. Everything was escaping him—a peculiar absent-mindedness. He could hardly remember how the funeral went.

As he thought about the funeral he felt puzzled and sad. That unfortunate woman. And now Nikki—a fresh paradox. Nikolai had been acting erratic and cold at the memorial service that morning.

That morning! Khoslov shifted his weight and the hammock started wobbling like a tender rowboat when you try to stand up. For a grown man with talent and sense Nikolai was at times a peculiar machine. Now this fuss over headstones. A stone is a stone. There was no need to jump on the Sunset View men, they were only performing their tasks. And now he was up there again, at the mortuary, wrangling over the little details, going over the bill, point by point. His mother's funeral, and he is checking the fine print.

Khoslov pulled the dead skin from his knuckle with his teeth. He spat it out. Peculiar. And each time he thought about it, he felt truly off-balance, surprised. A man lives with a woman like Anna and begins to expect it, the sickness. Like a radio with static. The end comes as a genuine surprise. Suddenly the routine of bad health is no longer a part of the house. Healthy people are dying like flies all the time, right and left. You expect a sick woman like Anna, confined to the house with her TV and capsules and quirks, to go on. A blank loss, like the empty surprise of the tongue when a tooth has come out.

Again he looked at the garden. Neglected, neglected. Coming apart at the seams everywhere. Rebelling. He recalled the advice of his father in St. Petersburg. Like a horse—that's a garden! Either you are the master, or it is the master! Someone has to remain in the saddle! Father understood flowers and plants. All year long they ate soup from his cabbages. And those stunning red beets!

7

He climbed out of the hammock and wandered about picking pale wisps of fur from his funeral suit. He felt too tired to change his clothes. He fingered the stems, pulled off petals, looked under the leaves. Thrips clung to the roses, diabrotica fed on the cucumber leaves. He almost stepped on a snail. He picked it up, took a look at the bottom of the shell, and flung the snail into Schwann's yard. All the snails in the area originated with Schwann, an obstetrician at Stanford who refused to spend money on pellets or sprays. An evangelical ecologist—in the back of his house Schwann had slowly created a jungle. At least seventeen Schwanns in or around Palo Alto, and this one, with his tin ear and his botanical anarchy, decides to set up his camp in the very next house. For a while Schwann had made caustic remarks about émigré aesthetes who declined to play an active role in the local political scene. Now the contact involved sullen silence. When he wasn't pulling out babies with his tongs, Schwann was tooling around the Peninsula in his Porsche from one political clambake to another. While his jungle kept breeding fresh snails. Seminars, city council, school board, a swinger of current events, always off in high gear and apparently totally blind to aesthetics. *Peter Grimes* is some kind of detergent to Schwann.

8

Khoslov sank to his knees. He checked the leaves of the yellow alyssum: earwigs, a regular cotillion. The earwigs were dancing out to enjoy the night air and chop into the few intact flowers and shrubs. He looked about helplessly. The garden was too much in motion tonight: it was full of the wrong kind of life. Mealybugs, caterpillars, whiteflies. All of this would take days to correct, maybe weeks. And the fleas on the dogs, who were gradually biting themselves into two nervous wrecks.

He began creeping about in the garden, pulling weeds,

nipping suckers and buds, and as he worked he forgot about his newly-pressed suit, about Anna and everything else. It was his one talent, a gift, and he knew it. A professional, a man who devotes his whole life to the making of things, must develop concentration. You must block some things out, push some things to the side. And he knew how to concentrate. Yes. *Like a spirited horse!* he thought, thinning the Michaelmas daisies and straightening the rice-paper plants.

9

Buster barked one short yip without arising. Alberto just yawned, scratched his ear. Nikolai was going noisily through the whole house closing windows and turning on lights. As he came out the side door, his left shoulder slightly up and his necktie in his hand, he looked tired. Almost sick. He ran his hand through his hair. It stuck out like the hair of a boy, a disorganized mop. He ignored the two pups. When he squinted his eyes acquired pouches.

Khoslov transfered a damp clump of weeds from one hand to the other. "Everything turned out okay?"

"I told them to give her a plaque." He looked at his father. "You're ruining your suit."

"We're surrounded by chaos—I don't know where to begin. You're staying home tomorrow?" The clump of weeds sailed into the basket in front of the garage. "You don't look very good."

"I look fine." He handed his father the Sunset View statement, coughed, climbed into the hammock and placed the tie over his eyes. "They're cheaper than headstones. With plaques they can run the big mowers right over the graves. Plaques are neater."

"Neater?" Khoslov stuffed the bill into his pocket without looking at it. "I'm going out of my head. Look at the agapanthus. And Schwann is sending his snails out again."

Figaro jumped up on Nikki's chest. Nikki grasped the cat by the scruff of the neck and flung him away. "What's with the windows?" He bent forward and unlaced his shoes, then leaned back. "The house is going to be invaded by moths."

"You don't understand air, Nikolai. The house needs some fresh air. Use your nose. You're not playing tomorrow?"

"Sure I'm playing." He clasped his hands behind his head and made a face. Like his father before age had forced him to retire and shift his interest to things of the soil, Nikolai played viola with the San Francisco Symphony. Third chair. "They're starting the Mahler tomorrow. It'll be a big mess." He crossed his long legs in the hammock and readjusted the tie over his eyes. "Why shouldn't I play?"

10

Khoslov went into the house with the dogs. Nikolai was taking it hard. He had wept at the funeral. Cracked jokes. Told Joad, the director, to hurry it up, he was dragging his feet. A peculiar machine.

The loaf was finally ready: a delicate brown crust glistening with mushrooms, half-buried and steaming. Khoslov leaned out the side door and looked at his son lying quietly in the hammock, the tie across his eyes like a blindfold. "Supper." He waited. "It's out of the oven. I baked us a meat loaf."

Nikki lay in the hammock. "Eat your meat loaf yourself," and he coughed. "Those Sunset View boys make me glad I'm alive." He lifted his necktie and looked at his father. "Do I look like I'm hungry for meat loaf?"

Khoslov turned up his palms to the pups. He started slicing the loaf. Already Nikki's hair was graying. Too early. From where was he getting this gray hair? Khoslov wiggled his wrist. For forty-five years he'd been sawing away on the viola, but never had he acquired that stoop which he saw in his son. Nikki had always neglected his body. Too much tobacco. Too much sherry at night. He was keeping unhealthy hours up in the city, poor Nikki, running around with that platform-shoe crowd, getting mixed up with heaven knows what. That Romanian guru and his ashram.

Khoslov leaned against the wall. The face-hinges moved. There he hangs off the ground, getting gray at his age and worrying about funeral plaques. And yet the screams of the Bavarian locomotives, the cold depots, the terrified eyes, the disgusting hotels wedged between permanent shadows, the columns of helmeted troops cranking up their field cycles—all these visions and sounds were so close to Khoslov, brought together in one awkward knot, just as close as the drone of the anchorman discussing the emergence of the New South on Schwann's TV next door.

No longer a straight line. Past and present were looping, creating a snarl.

11

Khoslov seated himself at the table and pried off a chunk of Siberian rye. He chewed silently, and as he chewed he divided a number of pieces of meat loaf and flicked them around. Figaro dragged his piece under the sink, where he guarded it, growling. The whippets knew better than to try to horn in. Because the meat loaf was still hot they didn't catch it in their mouths but allowed it to cool on the floor. As he ate he glanced up at the box of metaldehyde for the sowbugs. It had somehow gotten in with the Rice Chex and cracker crumbs and Chef Boy-Ar-Dee. A bizarre scene slid into his mind: metaldehyde and crumbs, side by side. He saw it wedged into a newspaper headline, somewhere on the second or third page, four stark lines:

Widowed Violist,
Tomcat and Whippets
In Suicide Pact:
Poisoned Meat Loaf

For the first time that evening he laughed. He opened a bottle of Schweppes. A tableau out of Gogol! The bottle cap bounced to the floor. He looked down at the floor.

That floor was something to look at: grease and pieces of meat, and now bent bottle caps. In the morning he'd start cleaning up the whole place, top to bottom. And the house needed flowers. Fresh flowers. More fresh air and sun. The place smelled like a furniture warehouse: things packed up and stored, not in use.

12

He felt sorry for Nikki, but the boy had a short memory. Especially now, with the funeral and the tedious sorting and putting away of her dresses and shoes, the quick scanning-through of her albums of clippings and snapshots—old, squiggly-cut photographs going clear back to their first days together in Riga—especially now Khoslov felt that his memory was in motion again. It curved and cut back like the paths he'd laid out in the garden. The fact was that they had been lucky. They had been lucky, or blessed. To escape from a terrible war takes some luck. Providence, perhaps. Of course like everyone else they knew it was coming, the war. They could smell it in the park benches in Riga. The holocaust. On the Rotterdam lamp posts. Wherever they stopped to give their concerts, the odor of crisis appeared to be hovering like cigarette smoke above the last couple of rows.

He thought back to Lucerne.

13

The idea to make their way to California had first come to them in Lucerne, and it came first to Nikki. Of course he wouldn't remember. They had taken Nikolai to see a program of Disney's cartoons in Lucerne, and he sighed and declared that he very much wanted to visit the land where the father of Donald Duck lived. First they laughed. Then they started to think. Calculate. Little Nikki was skinny and tended to twitch. Nervous tics. He seemed old for his age. Finally they committed themselves to the idea of the trip. They would try.

It was all hook and crook, scraping money together wherever a concert could be arranged—Zurich, Munich, Dortmund—Anna on the piano, the father and son on the strings, THE KHOSLOV FAMILY TRIO, and they promised themselves, he and Anna, no more harried suitcase life, no more grimy hotels where a boy couldn't play, where the lobbies were full of unsavory men wearing knickers. Nikki mustn't become a small talented freak in a black velvet suit. California—yes. In San Francisco there was a first-rate orchestra paying big money, and a World's Fair in the middle of the Bay on an island entirely constructed by man, and glittering parks full of palm trees and tropical fowl where the natives lay down on the grass and took baths in the sun.

They had sailed from Copenhagen in July, and the *Pilsudski,* they heard later, had met a German torpedo on the return run.

14

Khoslov opened a drawer and took out a flashlight. The knots that we tie are peculiar knots. He slipped the flashlight into his pocket and began teasing the dogs with fresh fragments of meat. Providence or plain luck—they had managed to flee and had slowly created their garden. One plant at a time. Out of death, out of the smoke, to all this. Alberto and Buster jumped up for the meat. Their jaws snapped.

15

Nikki lay in the hammock and fingered the bridge of his nose. Figaro had climbed up the littleleaf linden, his favorite tree, and was now on Schwann's roof. The night seemed to be getting unstuck at the edges, as though pasted on quickly and starting to curl. There was only a cut of a moon, a small gash without light, and the two dogs prowled silently through the lush garden, their ribs lighting up whenever they crossed the rectangle of light coming from the kitchen window, then again disappearing back into the black. Sinking down to his knees, Khoslov aimed his flashlight at the patches of quack grass and meadow fescue which were gradually strangling the lawn. He crept on all fours, as though trying to hunt down the pincers and hooked mandibles spiking into the life he had placed in this soil. The insatiable choppers and damp suction cups. Red and yellowish spores had disfigured the iris. He would have to yank out the diseased plants, make a fire and burn them.

Nikki coughed. "Can't you lay off?"

"Tell the bugs to lay off."

16

Khoslov glanced at the hammock but aimed the light elsewhere. It was really for him, all this crawling about on all fours. Years of crawling around, pulling weeds, digging holes. That was mainly for him, to make up for the black velvet suit and the curls dancing over his ears. Just in case he'd forgotten. That's right.

Nikki kept coughing. He was definitely smoking too much. Late hours and the odor of pot constantly and a Romanian holy man who charges high fees. Dear Lord. Khoslov continued to crawl about in the dark, like a fourth animal on the prowl. Certain things are beyond explanation, he thought. There is no lexicon. For a moment he froze. From sheer habit. He listened.

Nothing. He kept forgetting.

He shone his light on the kennel. Upstairs and downstairs, both inside and out, she had been lacking in health. Some of it had been real, some of it in the head. Nowhere else. Some diseases begin in the brain and work down. Allergies, rashes, long fits of sneezing, the pain in the throat, running eyes. All psychosomatic. The whippets appeared side by side and cocked their ears. He shone the light at their faces. Intelligent eyes.

And here was the truth: four bright eyes blinking back through the dark. She simply had no understanding of animals, of small living things. With the animals it began. She said "allergies" and "pollen" and gave this explanation and that explanation, but it boiled down to small living things. The first time he brought home a kitten for Nikki she hammered her fist until the window glass shook. Flea breeders, manure machines—animals made a clean house unclean, there were worms in their feces, microbes in their mouths. How can floors be kept clean when they leave their pawprints on the floors?

17

And so the sneezes and headaches began to appear. Like the weeds on the lawn. Nikki lay silently in the hammock. What was he twisting around in his mind? Had they come to the land of perpetual sun to exist in an ersatz environment, in a world scrubbed of motion and warmth? Disinfected? Did the dismal hotels and the suitcases make way for this? Like invalids in oxygen tents?

Of course she had allergies. Allergies are no joke. He was not an insensitive man. When an allergy strikes, certain steps must be taken. Very well—so the animals stay outside. All agreed. He built the barn for the dogs. And the flowers. All right—no flowers in the house, except those made of plastic or straw. Sanity, order, cleanliness. Okay.

But the simple truth was that she had no understanding of them. Animals she didn't understand. Little bones under skin and warm fur were repellent to her. Plants were better, plants could be controlled, kept in place, but they, too, became ugly and gave off pungent odors—all those soggy and limp tubes and underground networks of slimy white roots.

More and more, her assortment of rashes and sores seemed to sink through her skin and come out at the tips of her fingers, leaving marks on the house. Her passion for cleanliness had gradually transformed itself into a stiff and habitual fear. Because the winds from the foothills brought dust to the house, the windows had to stay shut. And so she banished herself from the flowers and plants in the garden which he had contrived for their son and suggested they change the whole scheme—they would put in a pool or a stone patio with a barbecue pit. He replied by installing an elegant border of senecio scaposus, a succulent plant growing fingerlike leaves with the texture of felt.

Somehow it had to be explained to her, and if that couldn't be done, it had to be demonstrated. You are either with life or against it. Draw the line. What's a home without small bowls of food on the floor? And only last month, when poor Schatzi, the spitz with the silvery coat, got run over by the idiot next door in his Porsche, she showed obvious relief. An unhealthy reaction. Negation. So he drove to the kennel and returned with Alberto and Buster, who came from the same litter and should never be parted—for aesthetic considerations, if for no other. She was a sensible woman. How well she had managed their business affairs on the tours. Item by item, with precision and care. Sooner or later she'd see that her various disorders were all triggered off by a catalogue of unfounded fears. She would learn to accept, then enjoy smells and noises and movement beyond her control. She would stop sterilizing her life, flicking switches, ON, OFF, changing channels at will, and her sickness would go with the false plastic flowers and the pictures of cute little kittens in baskets which she snipped out of magazines—to prove that she, too, had a fondness for God's little things.

So it went. He struggled to force her to tear herself out of her aluminum-foil world, an endless and almost unmodulated series of trivial routines, all neatly partitioned, quick-frozen, dished up in disposable trays. She, in turn, padded around the house in her slippers, tightening all the faucets and screws, filling in all the cracks, saturating the bathroom with Air-Wick, until finally she simply established herself in front of her color TV, while he spent most of his time with the pollen and the germs and the dust from the hills.

18

"I'm going to bed," Nikki said suddenly. He'd been

weeping in the hammock and his eye pouches looked bad. As Nikki walked to the house Buster grazed against his leg. Nikki gave him a kick that sent him yowling with one hind paw up in the air. Khoslov remained outside.

Something clattered and fell in the kitchen. Nikki grumbled to himself. He had apparently slid on the grease-covered floor and knocked over a chair. Khoslov could hear him going up to his room. He kept coughing as he climbed up the stairs.

With the help of the flashlight Khoslov continued to work in the garden. It was cold now, and he felt the dirt on his knees. Chalk off one fancy funeral suit. Schwann came outside with the garbage sack and emptied the garbage and went back inside.

19

Khoslov stood in the middle of the garden and switched off the light. The great box of darkness slammed down. He called to the cat. You begin with a parcel of nothing, a blank plot of dirt, and begin to create. Father's Petersburg beets were like that: bona fide calculated creations. He switched the light on. The beam seemed to be ricocheting away from the flowers and plums. Everything in the garden was made of fine metal and locked in a pattern with levers and clamps. Figaro reappeared. A man could dismantle it all, piece by piece, and refurbish it, scrape off the rust and give the whole business a fresh coat of paint. It was very well made.

Holding Figaro in his arms, Khoslov circled around the damp hammock and entered the house. The pups preceded him into the kitchen. *I am sorry for Nikki,* he thought. For a moment he felt a brief dip of regret. *He is sure I was driving her into the ground with this life.*

He let Figaro leap from his arms to the table and locked the side door. The dogs trotted around licking grease from the floor. Khoslov unbuttoned his vest. It had been a good loaf. The meat-spattered linoleum floor, and the dishes, the squashed cake, the bottles, the overturned chair gave the kitchen the look of a slightly disreputable room in which someone had just held a banquet.

Wachtmann's Cubes

6:40 A.M. Wachtmann glared at the parrot and tried to recapture the chords he had seen in his dream. He kicked off his blankets. The cloth had slipped from the top of the cage and hung down like a tongue. Beckmesser was rattling his throat and adjusting his wings. His right eye was completely closed now.

Wachtmann pushed himself out of the bed. He threw the plastic cup into the trash bag and limped to the window. Again the window was stuck. The fog sliced off the top half of Telegraph Hill, as though someone had pulled down a shade. He could hear the foghorns on San Francisco Bay. Downstairs in the kitchen Tsugami was chopping the kidneys for the cat. Wachtmann put all his weight on the frame. The window came down with a crash. Tsugami stopped chopping.

He climbed on the stool and unfastened the cloth from the cage. When he offered Beckmesser the tip of his finger, the parrot retreated one hop. Another long rattle. It was not a good rattle. Wachtmann listened. The rattle was bad. He climbed down from the stool and limped over to the table. As Beckmesser got worse, he seemed to be expanding in some curious way. Filling up more of the room. Wachtmann picked up the pen. Once again, he was seeing the chords he had seen in his dream, an arrangement of cubes. Beckmesser lifted one foot and the cubes changed their shape. Wachtmann set the pen down. Tsugami was chopping again.

6:56 A.M. He adjusted the straps around his legs. The ache in his joints came and went, as though someone were twisting a dial. When you strain for the notes, they don't come; when you finally give up, they slide back in the dead of the night. The cat in the kitchen was crying for meat. Wachtmann counted the splats as the kidney chunks hit the linoleum.

Again a long rattle.

Maybe Beckmesser had picked up a virus from the cat. Cats carried toxic dust in their fur. Every night he could hear the cat growling about in the corridors, clawing the carpets, then crouching and scratching at things as Tsugami worked the sewing machine in the bedroom and assaulted his ears with her infernal Hokkaido laments.

He forced himself into the green uniform that Finley had issued to him. A man couldn't work in this house any more: cats and sewing machines and Tsugami's flat, sorrowful face. The shirt was stiff with starch. The zipper on the pants seemed to be stuck. Finally it gave. The legs of the pants were four inches too long. As he was rolling up the pants he could see the cubes starting to surface again, coming out of the little gas heater, but before he could get to his desk Beckmesser hopped to the left and they sank out of sight.

7:10 A.M. Tsugami was wiping her hands on a towel when he limped down the stairs with the Cannonball manual in his hand. She had painted her eyelids again and was wearing that blouse he had bought her a couple of years ago, when she took him to see *Turandot* at the Opera House. He could hear the TV in the living room: voices without human tones. She folded the towel. "I keep reminding you about that window. You don't listen to me."

"Fix the window," he said.

"You'll break the glass one of these days." She went into the kitchen. "You've broken enough things already around here." She hesitated. "Breakfast."

"No breakfast. And keep the door closed to my room."

She stood before the stove, her back to him. "Eat an egg."

"No eggs." This impossible woman. He had given as much as he could. There was no more to give.

"You can't start a new job without something inside—you are not a young man." She poured him some coffee. "Something more than that stuff you were drinking last night. I can smell it from here."

"I don't need any eggs. All I need is some privacy and peace."

She did a thing with her neck, like a chicken. "It'll happen again—you are going to tear yourself down." She set the cup on the counter. "I don't know why you're doing these things. I have stood behind you for five years. Why are you treating me like this?"

He went to the front door, the Cannonball manual rolled up in his hand. She followed him. "What did I do to you?" She waited. "Are you thinking of moving out again?"

"The cat," he warned, pushing Tsugami aside. "The house is full of toxic dust." He went out into the fog.

8:05 A.M. Finley was dragging the tire display from the lube room to the front of the station. The transistor radio in the office was giving the traffic report: heavy flow southbound on the Golden Gate Bridge. The Cannonball sign floated high in the fog.

"You're early," the manager grunted, dragging the tire display to the pumps. He glanced at the manual. "How'd it go?"

Wachtmann handed him the manual. "I can't follow the technical terms. There is no glossary." He put his hands in his pockets. "This uniform is too big."

Finley took the manual into the office and came out dragging a rack filled with oil additives. "They don't come any smaller than that—it's the best I could do. You're awfully short, you know. Come in here for a minute."

They went into the lube room. Wachtmann glanced around: a work table with wrenches and ratchets. Against the wall, a pegboard with fanbelts. Radiator hoses.

"We've got to take count," Finley said, tearing open a carton. Fuses. He handed him a pencil. Someone had been chewing on it. "Write this down."

"There was no listing of terms," Wachtmann said. "What is *torque?*"

Finley studied the carton of fuses, as though trying to remember what they were. "I'll tell Harry to give you a hand."

Wachtmann noticed the manager's hair. It was brittle and thin, but carefully styled. There were two boils on the back of his neck. "The manual kept referring to *torque.*"

"Wait a minute," Finley said. "What happened to your cap?"

Wachtmann's hand went to his head. Suddenly he was tasting last night's rum. It felt like a clot in the back of his throat.

"Didn't I issue you a cap?"

"You didn't give me a cap."

Finley went to the back room, where the employees had their lockers, and returned with a green baseball cap. It bore the Cannonball emblem in crimson and black. The cap slid over Wachtmann's ears like a helmet.

"I am not a mechanic," Wachtmann said. "I explained that to you."

"Right. That's right."

"I told you I'm willing to learn. But I can't be expected to—."

"Well, that's right." The manager kept nodding. Why was he nodding like that, with the boils on the back of his neck? "I'm trying to help. You'll do fine." His eyes changed their shape. A Dodge van with a CB antenna coasted up to the pumps. "I'm really trying to help. I can see things in you."

8:11 A.M. Wachtmann was pulling the nozzle out of the van when Harry roared up on his Honda. A beefy boy with red hands. He climbed off the bike. "Well, hello." He unzipped his ski jacket. "That cap's kind of big, isn't it?"

Wachtmann began cleaning the windshield. He strained, but he couldn't reach the top of the glass. The CB radio was crackling. The braces cut into his thighs.

"Keep an eye on him, Harry," the manager said. "Show him how everything works."

Wachtmann ran the credit card through the printer. He limped to the front of the van and wrote down its license. On the bumper: I FOUND IT! The CB radio made peculiar squawks as the driver sat back and stared into the fog.

Harry led Wachtmann into the lube room. "You've got to learn to solicit," he said.

Wachtmann looked up at him.

"*Solicit,*" Harry said. "Look here." He pulled on one of the drawers. Wiper blades. "The gas sells itself. There's no problem with gas. What you've got to do—you've got to push these here blades, and the pressure caps and hoses and plugs, things like that. You've got to remind people their hoses and blades need replacing. It's a service to them. You don't want them driving around in the fog with worn-out wiper blades." He pulled a card from his shirt pocket and held it in front of Wachtmann's eyes: TEN SURE-FIRE WAYS OF INCREASING YOUR SALES IN A HURRY.

Finley stepped into the lube room. "All set?"

Harry slipped the card back in his pocket. "We were waiting for you."

Finley's eyes changed their shape. Wachtmann tried to ignore the transistor radio—a ballad about a diesel truck cutting through Kansas in the middle of the night. It wasn't clear if the singer was a woman or a man.

"All right," Finley said. "Let's just take a look over here."

He pushed a red button marked UP and the grease rack clattered up, but with hitches, as though something in the mechanism were starting to slip, and in the back room the compressor began hissing out air, and the rack shivered and froze, less than two feet from the floor.

"It's stuck," Harry said. His hands hung at his sides. "That's as high as she goes."

Wachtmann stared at the rack. Finley scrunched himself down to his size. "It's been freezing like that for a week and a half, and it's costing us big revenue. Every day I lose out on at least eight, nine lubes. Half a dozen oil changes. It really adds up. I keep waiting for the maintenance crew to come in and repair it—."

"They're on strike," Harry said.

"They're on strike?"

"Might take weeks."

"Either I wait, or I find a good man who can work at that height without breaking his back."

Wachtmann backed away from the rack.

"That's why I need somebody, uh, small."

"You didn't mention the rack," Wachtmann said.

"Well, it's perfectly safe. It's just cramped under there."

"You knew I was desperate for money! You told me—."

"Hold on!" Finley said. "Settle down!"

"My parrot is sick! The landlady sucks my soul dry! Toxic dust in the air! You're taking advantage of me!"

Finley lowered his voice. "I'm not taking advantage of you! What do you mean, I'm taking advantage of you? You think I'm in love with these pumps? You've had some bad times. Fine. You think you're alone? You need money? Everybody needs money! I'm putting my woman through school! What the hell are you talking about?"

The bell rang. Wachtmann limped out to the pumps. Harry followed. "I don't think that was right. He's really trying to help. He told me. He said he sees something special in you."

Wachtmann was silent.

"What's the matter with your legs?" Harry asked.

"Braces."

"How come?"

"A disease."

9:50 A.M. The first lube job was a Chevy wagon with scratches on its doors and a wire compartment for dogs. Finley pushed the UP button and the rack shivered and froze at the usual place. They slid underneath. Finley drained the oil into a pan and explained about the fittings. "Here. Here. Over here. This one here. Back in there." He shifted his position. "All right. Let's get the oil filter off."

Wachtmann reached for the filter. It was hot.

"Not like that," Finley said. He handed him the filter wrench. "Always use the right tool."

As Wachtmann was slipping the wrench around the filter he caught a glimpse of the cubes. He yanked.

"Not so hard," Finley said. "Take it slow. It'll come." He squirmed out from under the grease rack and went to the office.

"It's stuck!" Wachtmann called out.

"Just go slow. It'll come." He was working an adding machine. "What's with your parrot, anyway?"

"He's sick."

"I know he's sick. What's the matter with him?"

"Toxic dust from the cat."

"Then get rid of the cat."

"The cat isn't my cat."

"I'd get rid of the cat anyway." More computations on the adding machine. "Why did you leave Amsterdam?"

"I completed my studies at the Conservatory."

"I mean why didn't you stay where you were?"

Wachtmann looked at the grime on his knuckles. "The desire for success."

Finley started tapping his feet. "What else did you study—besides the piano?"

"Composition."

"What else?"

"I didn't—." He yanked on the wrench and the filter was suddenly loose. The oil flowed over his hands, down his wrists.

Finley came out of the office and knelt down. "Oh boy!" He threw him a rag. "It's okay. Don't worry about it."

"I need another cloth."

Finley threw him another. "There you go."

Wachtmann wiped the oil from his hands. Finley watched. He was crouching on all fours. "My shirt is a mess," Wachtmann said. "Look at these sleeves!"

Finley kept looking at him thoughtfully.

"What is it?" Wachtmann asked.

"You look like a character out of a play," Finley said. "All you need is a knife."

Wachtmann was silent.

"I'm really intrigued by the stage," Finley said.

"I haven't been to the theater in years."

"It's an unusual world," Finley said. "It gets right to the point."

6:12 P.M. As they were both washing up, Finley announced he would buy him a quick cup of coffee at the corner cafeteria. His wife Emma was waiting for him—they were going to a party—and she'd certainly want to meet the new man on the team. Emma, he said, was a people-person. She liked people. She liked to cultivate new friends. She was going into social welfare work and meeting people was one of her natural gifts.

The manager handed him a bundle wrapped in brown paper. Clean uniforms. "That's as small as they come, I'm afraid. Maybe you can get your landlady to alter them." He began changing his clothes. "They might shrink in the wash. I don't know. You can leave your cap here."

Wachtmann stared at the front of his shirt. "No coffee tonight. I'm too tired and Beckmesser needs food."

"You're pretty fond of your parrot, aren't you?"

"He brings me both comfort and grief."

Finley slipped into an embroidered Mexican peasant blouse. Instead of buttons it had pegs. "I'll drop you off at your place on the way to the party."

"Some other night."

"One quick cup."

6:18 P.M. The cafeteria smelled of floor wax and stew, and the faded photomurals of San Francisco were covered with miscellaneous notices. An elderly bus boy with knots in his shoestrings was reading a religious tract in the corner. Two Yellow Cab drivers were sitting opposite each other, spooning clam chowder into their mouths. Directly behind them was Emma, a redheaded woman with an attaché case.

Emma had a bright smile and thick bones. Genuine. As Finley went to the counter for coffee, she gave Wachtmann an amusing account of the statistics exam she had struggled with that morning. Her eyes fluttered like valves. Statistics were certainly strange, she observed. They reminded her of hired hit men. Wachtmann agreed that statistics were strange.

Finley returned with the coffee and picked up the sugar dispenser. "So how'd it go?" He let the sugar flow into his cup in a long steady stream.

She described the statistics exam.

Finley shook his head. "Sophistry." He handed the sugar dispenser to Wachtmann. "It's almost over now. She's got one more semester to go."

Wachtmann folded his hands. "Then you'll have your degree?"

Emma smiled.

"An accomplishment," Wachtmann said.

"He was there every step of the way," Emma said, removing a strand of thread from Finley's sleeve. "He's been very supportive."

Finley lowered his eyes. Emma picked up her cup. There was something between them. Wachtmann wanted to leave.

"Feel like talking?" Finley asked. His eyes were still aimed at the floor.

Wachtmann blinked at him.

Emma gave Wachtmann's hand a light pat. "Don't take him too seriously. He gets into soul-searching at the end of the day—he says it's his dramatic instinct."

Finley leaned forward. "Something happened to you."

"Something happened to me?"

"You're a gifted man. It shows in your eyes. I can see it in your hands."

Wachtmann slipped his hands under the table.

"That's right," Finley said. "You were trained at the Conservatory. The day you came in with the want-ad I found myself thinking: *Something's happened to him. He needs help.*"

"Everybody needs help," Wachtmann said.

"Why the pumps?"

"It's a job."

"It might help if you talked about it."

Emma seemed to be backing away silently.

Wachtmann stared at the large photomural, but instead of the mural he saw Beckmesser staring at him with his single good eye.

He spoke quickly, the way people speak when they want to disentangle themselves. He described the early recitals in Amsterdam, the minor successes, the move to New York and its neighborhood orchestras, the gradual typecasting, the shift to L.A. and the slippage as he bounced from one film studio to the next, and then the live TV shows and the cocktail lounges and the pizza parlors that needed a piano for their Buster Keaton flicks. He didn't mention his daughter or wife, or the bottles of rum, or the last sullen years under Tsugami's roof.

"When the disease of the bone settled in, I could no longer play properly."

"I've been watching your eyes," Finley said. "You're still fighting to be what you are." He turned to Emma. "He hasn't sold out."

"What are you doing these days?" Emma asked.

"I've been trying to compose."

"Any luck?"

"I see chords in my mind. They have different shapes. The ideas are hard to get down." He slapped the top of his head. Again, there was Beckmesser's eye. "Everything has to come out of here."

"You must've had some kind of medical coverage," Emma said. For a moment she sounded professional.

Wachtmann shook his head. "I was negligent about practical things. I felt I was beyond such concerns."

"That was very unfortunate," Emma said.

"I regret it today."

"Sit tight," Emma said. "Be right back." She arose and went ponderously to the rest room. The bus boy nodded to her.

"A good woman," Wachtmann said.

"Well, she has a good heart," Finley said. "She'll do well in her field. She is really sincere."

Wachtmann thought of his wife. An elaborate machine. Gears and springs.

"Emma's practical," Finley said. "I'm like you. You may find that hard to believe. I saw it right away. We have a lot in common. She's got both of her feet on the ground. I want to get the hell out of this job. She keeps reminding me about all the years I've invested in Cannonball Gas—and she's right. I can move up to a desk job pretty soon. They think very highly of me."

"You're a good manager."

"The economy is bad," Finley said. "We were talking about it last night. Jobs are terribly scarce."

"Very scarce," Wachtmann said.

"It's depressing."

When Emma returned from the rest room her hands were still wet. "No towels. George said they ran out." She bent over Wachtmann protectively. "You're coming to the party with us."

"Not tonight," Wachtmann said.

"Well, it's very informal. Just some friends. You've got to have something to eat."

"The landlady gives me my meals."

Finley got out of his chair. "I promised to drive him home."

"You're not eating enough," Emma said. She took Wachtmann's hand. "Come along."

6:44 P.M. Wachtmann slid around on the cluttered back seat of Finley's Volvo wagon. Torn theater magazines, a crepe-soled shoe, playbills, the *Chronicle.* At his feet was a cardboard model of a set: a fourposter on a platform and a hidden door, made to look like a part of the wall, and some steps going down. The fourposter was coming apart.

Emma noticed him looking at it. "He's so good with his hands."

"An original design."

"He's made dozens of them."

Finley shifted to second. They were starting to climb a steep hill. "*The Madwoman of Chaillot.*"

"He enjoys making sets," Emma said.

Wachtmann leaned forward. "You've made *dozens* of these?"

"Watch the hill," Emma said.

7:03 P.M. He clutched at his bundle and bowed to the hostess, a benign-looking woman in a t-shirt and jeans. Finley had disappeared down the hall. As Emma led Wachtmann to the buffet table she introduced him around. Her friends worked with ghetto children, with the aged, with addicts, with the indigent in Hunter's Point. One woman specialized in therapy for the deaf. Emma loaded food on his plate. He withdrew to a corner and proceeded to eat.

Emma went to the kitchen. On the couch slumped a girl with a very sweet face, like the face of a child, but her voice was all wrong for such delicate eyes. Emma reappeared with a tumbler of wine. Wachtmann thought of Tsugami's incessant harranguing about the rum bottles he brought to his room. He accepted the wine.

"I'll get you more herring," she said.

"I've had plenty of herring," he said.

She sat down. "I want him to be a success. I want him to be happy. You understand that."

Wachtmann nodded and tasted the wine.

"He isn't happy," she said. She paused. "There's a shadow on him. You notice how he withdraws."

"A shadow?"

"He keeps yearning for things he can't have."

Wachtmann was silent.

"You've heard him yourself. He keeps talking about that theatrical world. We buy season tickets. It isn't enough. He would like to design and direct."

"He has gifts."

"It's becoming an obsession with him."

"He's ambitious."

"He's out of his head. He has no formal training. It'd take him years to get anywhere. There's no work to be had. Where is he going to direct? *Who* is he going to direct? Qualified people with years of experience are looking for jobs. They've got no place to go. They end up pumping gas. Look at you."

"It's a dilemma," he said.

"Try to eat." She pushed herself up and went back to her friends.

Wachtmann listened to them. Laughter and exclamations, as though someone were stirring the room with a ladle. He glanced out the window. An oil tanker seemed to be nailed to the middle of the bay. Alcatraz was aglow. Maybe he should have phoned Tsugami. A cable car clanged down the street and tipped itself over the hill. She was not a bad woman. He felt sorry for her. Tsugami had always been patient and long-suffering. But he didn't like feeling indebted to her. She'd assured him there would be no strings if he stayed without paying any rent. That was three years ago, and he'd kept himself free of her pressures and hooks. The woman thrived on rebuffs. She solicited them. Did he have to come home to her steamed vegetables every night? Let her wait.

He watched as a striking young couple appeared side by side, the woman's ash-blonde hair in a single long braid down her back. Her partner had very deep eyes and looked Lebanese. Maybe Egyptian. Wachtmann followed the woman with his eyes as he finished the wine. He tried catching the sound of her voice, but there was too much noise. He went to the kitchen for more wine.

8:47 P.M. No more chianti, he reminded himself as he walked carefully down the hall to the bathroom. The bathroom was occupied. He turned into the study. Finley was lying on the couch. His eyes were closed and he was balancing a half-empty glass on his chest. The radio was on. Wachtmann listened: *Wozzeck,* the last scene. Against the wall stood an old upright. Someone had repainted it in rainbow colors. Wachtmann sat down on the hassock and listened to the *Wozzeck*.

When the opera was over, Finley sat up and exhaled. "I was wondering how long you could take it out there."

"They're good people," Wachtmann said.

"Yes, they are."

Wachtmann went to the bathroom.

9:02 P.M. When he returned to the study he saw that Finley

had brought a second glass. He was unscrewing the cap from the bottle of bourbon. The radio was off.

"I saw a striking blonde woman out there," Wachtmann said. "The one with the braid. Do you know who she is?"

"How would I know who she is?" Finley handed him his glass. "I've been in here all night."

"She came with a dark man. Egyptian."

"I don't know who she is."

"She reminded me of my wife," Wachtmann said.

Finley looked surprised, as though he were seeing Wachtmann from a different perspective.

They drank.

9:40 P.M. "You haven't said anything about your wife," Finley said.

"There is nothing to say." Wachtmann could hear the toilet flushing. "She climbed up, I slid down."

"What is she doing these days?"

"Los Angeles Philharmonic. The flute section. First chair."

"That's pretty good."

"That's very good."

They drank silently for a while.

"How long were you married?" Finley asked.

"Less than two years."

"How long have you been living alone?"

"A long time." Tsugami didn't count.

"Was she unfaithful?"

"I don't know. I don't think so."

They drank.

"You did bad things to her?" Finley asked.

Wachtmann didn't reply.

"Why?" Finley asked.

"I don't know."

"You're a frustrated man," Finley said.

10:06 P.M. Finley's voice had grown cold. "You abuse women who love you. Correct?"

Wachtmann tried to ignore him.

"Did you have any kids?" Finley asked.

"A girl."

"How old is your daughter?"

"Twelve—thirteen." He looked up at the ceiling. "She's thirteen."

Finley was twisting one of the pegs on his Mexican blouse. He talked into his glass. "Well, you can't blame your wife."

"I have never blamed my wife."

"Women need consideration," Finley said. "A woman has to have respect. She can't be treated like—."

"My wife had plenty to object to," Wachtmann agreed.

"Well, I imagine she did."

"She objected to failure," Wachtmann said. He wiggled his glass. "And to this."

11:10 P.M. "Play something for me," Finley said.

Wachtmann wiped his mouth. "I can't play."

Finley shuffled out to the hallway and brought in a chair and placed it in front of the gaudy piano. "Go on. Play."

Wachtmann's forefinger struck a chipped key. "It won't come any more. I pushed everything else to the side." He sat down at the keyboard. The bright colors were hurting his head. "I can't get it to come."

"You can play," Finley said.

Wachtmann struck a soft chord. Then another. He eased himself into fragments . . . loose ends. Finley took the high-intensity lamp from the desk and set it on top of the upright. He plugged it in.

"I don't need the lamp," Wachtmann said.

Finley switched on the light. Wachtmann saw his hands dipping into the circle of white.

As he played he found himself edging again towards the

cubes he had seen in his dream. He heard Beckmesser's rattle. He stopped and rubbed his fingers together. Again he went after the cubes. They broke off as the rattle increased. The manager sat down next to him on the hassock. He was holding his head in his hands. Wachtmann went back to the cubes. His knuckles were blue against the white of the keys. He could see the cubes clearly, to the left of the parrot. Beckmesser was working his talons. Wachtmann closed his eyes. As he struggled to fix the true shape of the cubes he heard voices behind him. Emma was in the hallway with some of her friends. They were discussing legislative reforms in Sacramento. The parrot cocked his head. The piano turned dead. The cubes slid out of sight.

Wachtmann stood up. Finley's eyes seemed inflamed. "Are you coming to work in the morning?"

Wachtmann steadied himself against the piano. "I don't know."

"Cannonball doesn't satisfy me," Finley said.

Wachtmann picked up his bundle. "You're looking for something to satisfy you?"

11:32 P.M. He started limping downhill to Columbus Avenue. The braces cut into his flesh. The bundle kept changing its shape in his arms.

North Beach tangled itself around him. He felt he was pushing through kelp. Young men were roaming about. The topless nightclubs were like smoking machines. He limped past a middle-aged man in a green leisure suit who was arguing with his wife. They were standing in front of an Adult Theater, and she was tired and wanted to go home, and he was angry because she was tired. Wachtmann felt dizzy, as though her weariness had gone into him. The woman said, *Go watch the show by yourself and I'll take a cab home,* and her husband said, *Man, that's so typical of you!*

Wachtmann was halfway across Columbus Avenue before

he realized that he was walking against the light. A car filled with Chinese youths slammed on its brakes. A truck blasted him with its horn.

12:08 A.M. As he was turning the corner that led to Tsugami's, he heard a low hissing behind him. He limped up the hill. All his life, since the earliest years, he had struggled for silence and space, but his privacy had brought him no peace. A street-cleaning truck spraying water drove past, its brushes revolving, sucking up dirt and debris.

His feet echoed on the stone steps leading to the front door. He pulled out his key and groped for the lock. The lock kept twisting away from his hand.

He was securing the chain on the front door when she came out of her room in her quilted white robe. Her black hair hung down like a hood. He had almost forgotten the way it hung down when she took out the pins. The cat pattered out of the kitchen, looked around, and withdrew.

Her face was like a sheet of paper. "Take a look at yourself."

He started to climb the stairs. He would deal with Tsugami in the morning. It had happened enough times before. He would eat some of her steamed vegetables and she'd leave him alone for a while.

"Why are you doing these things?"

He stopped, then continued on to the top of the stairs. The cubes were somewhere up there, in his room. He opened the door and climbed up on the stool and peered into the cage. Beckmesser stared back at him.

All Terminations Begin in the Mind

I

Feb. 18, 1974–Feb. 25, 1974

MONDAY. Stuck to my promise and hauled the boat over the summit yesterday in spite of the hammering in my head. Laura did well with the tiller until we got snagged in the kelp and the whitecaps appeared. The gusts and the tide pushed us steadily into the reefs. Made Alex crouch down in the cockpit and managed to slide through the kelp with the centerboard up.

We tied up for a while at the end of the Santa Cruz pier and roamed about on the Boardwalk in our wet sneakers, the booths clattering in the wind. Alex was sullen because the Skee-Ball concession was closed. I kept seeing Constanza everywhere.

The gusts gradually subsided and Laura brought us back into the harbor on a single clean tack which eluded the worst of the swells. After we got the boat back on the trailer Alex asked if we could hike down the tracks to Capitola again. I said no.

As we were heading back over the summit Laura's mood quickly changed. She complained I was weaving, and why did I have to bring rum on the boat, and she'd appreciate it if somebody uttered an occasional word, my silence was getting everyone tense, etc. I told her to kindly restrain herself, she was getting on my nerves. She gave me a laugh and said oh boy, Constanza has done it again, hasn't she? I threw her a look. She stared out the window the rest of the way.

The hammering got worse when we reached Palo Alto.

Alex helped me unhitch the trailer and quietly withdrew. I had a cup of coffee with Claire and observed that the children are acting distant again, they don't want to connect any more. She said what do you know about that—has your girl friend run off with her dog? I drove to the apartment and swam forty laps in the pool.

I was finishing dinner when Constanza finally decided to call. She sounded defensive, and the jabs about my emotional miserliness were rehearsed. I didn't ask where she was hiding herself this time. She said Joe, you'd better get your head straight—your staggering into my cottage after falling out of that tree was just a little bit more than I'm willing to take. I said it wasn't exactly my fault that the branch broke on me. I could hear Waldo whimpering, and the sound of foghorns. She was probably in San Francisco again. We ran out of words. She said she wasn't feeling very well and hung up. Uneasy twisting all night.

THURSDAY. Colder. Got myself up at 5:30 A.M. and drove past her cottage. Still empty. Sparrow said I looked awful and explained during lunch how I could stabilize my life. I said I wasn't sure where she was hiding herself and the dog, but it sounded like San Francisco. He said Joey, you're scrambling your psychic field flow—you owe it to yourself to forget about these women, all of them, and especially Constanza, they are all obvious disasters for you; I keep telling you to plug yourself into my Thursday night group energy, get in touch with your inner-space needs. He rummaged about in his box and dug out the brochure: self-hypnosis with biofeedback and the Tai Chi Chuan. I said Sparrow, please leave me alone. He said Joe, your main problem is simple: the more you abuse people, the harder you hang on to them. I got up to leave. He said listen, I've watched you for seventeen years, two divorces, a daughter and son, crazy ladies who play games with you—you can take, but you've never learned how to let go, better come to the session tonight. I promised I'd certainly try hard to make it tonight and escaped. I thought about Constanza waltzing up Telegraph Hill with the terrier on his fifteen foot leash and decided to skip the finance committee staff session. That fifteen foot leash says it all about her.

SATURDAY. When I drove past the cottage around midnight she was there in the bedroom, unpacking, her face almost yellow, the circles under her eyes even worse than before. Waldo was shivering on the bed. He had made himself sick nosing vermin in one of the alleys off Grant Avenue.

I helped her unpack, and then she brought out the rum. She kept fingering the scar on her cheek and went into the old monologue about my trying to stash away chunks of the past for some private future use, which accounts for my continuous distance and emotional duplicity, etc. I said Constanza, I've never met a person yet who doesn't have some kind of past, even Sparrow has a past, and what about all those phone calls from poor old Patrick in the middle of the night? She said Joseph, your past seems to stick to your skin—everywhere you go you leave fingerprints and tracks, and it was really degrading the way you dragged yourself back to my cottage with your shirt practically torn in half and the blood on your hand, what's the matter with you, scrambling up trees in the dark to check up on a woman who kept you hungry and anxious for over three years. I said the branch broke on me and I'm tired of this, so let's just let it go for a while. She said please take the dog for a walk.

I took Waldo out on his fifteen foot leash. The tree incident started pressing on me. I kept seeing Julie's face, the way she stared out the window at me just before the branch broke. When I returned Constanza informed me she had picked up a new yeast infection. I said fine. Waldo kept snaffling all night.

MONDAY. To Sausalito yesterday for Laura's birthday dinner. She's fifteen today. When I asked her what she wanted for her birthday she requested I stop smoking and lighten up on the juice. I didn't think Constanza would come after all the invisible duelling between the two of them, but she popped up at the apartment just as we were leaving with some flowers and a gift, so I had to invite her along. She was overflowing with tender recollections and kept hugging dear Laura, who grew more and more tense. Constanza said Joseph, there's been so much closeness between all of us, even little Alex, I wish you had brought him along, so much misunderstanding and pain, especially those bittersweet weekends when we'd all be jammed together in that little bungalow in Capitola. Laura said since when have you been fond of Alex? Constanza ignored that and gave her the turquoise ring she had gotten from Patrick just before they had split—she said it had meaning for her that went way beyond words.

The dinner went fine at first—except that Constanza started objecting to the scampi being cemented to the shell, and the band struck her as just a lot of fraudulent noise, an overkill of Chicano brass and some African cowbells and reeds. I asked Laura to dance. She shook her head. I asked Constanza. She said the infection was bothering her and turned to scrutinize the glittery crowd at the bar—she characterized them as turkeys from nowhere who've just discovered platform shoes.

We edged into silence. When Laura went off to the ladies' room Constanza informed me that I'm still trying to alleviate my guilt feelings about the divorce by bowing and scraping to her—she said your fawning is really deplorable. I asked what did I do. She said Joseph, the trouble with you is you don't even know what you do—you've been jumping through so many hoops for your wives and your kids you'll be sprouting a tail pretty soon. I reminded her of the terrier that

Patrick had supposedly sent to obedience school: five years old, he still dribbles his load on the rug and gets wiped with a cloth. I said Christ, look at you: you subsist on food stamps and unemployment checks and keep ruining the dog's stomach with cans of smoked oysters. She gave me her Big Trouble smile. Drove back to the Peninsula with the radio on, not a word.

TUESDAY. A rambling phone call from Constanza in the middle of the night. She said my withdrawals have become so reflexive I'm not even aware when I'm pulling away. I said what are you talking about. She said Joseph, how many lives have you tarnished because you need to reduce your whole world to a handful of characters you can control? Laura is on her guard against you, Alex fades out of sight, and you don't even have the decency to store the sailboat in your carport: after all these years and all your shabby betrayals, you're still using Claire's garage, as though part of you has to continue on Hopkins Street, leaving its mark.

I said listen, Claire has never complained about the boat staying in the garage, and it's certainly better than letting it bleach in the sun. She said right, that's a perfect example of how you manipulate women and make them feel glad for the bonds. I thanked her for the insights and left the phone off the hook.

II

Feb. 26, 1974–Apr. 2, 1974

MONDAY. Overcast. She appears and I push her away, she withdraws and I want to find some way of punishing her. She informs me she's thinking of driving to Portland to minister to Patrick, he's been getting his astral projections again. I tell her to go.

Phoned Laura last night. I asked her to kindly explain what's been gnawing at her. She said Dad, the mist around you is so thick I can hardly get through any more—the only time you emerge is when Constanza shows up with her cameras and that neurotic terrier, and then you block out everything else, I don't even exist, and as soon as she leaves you go back to the mist. I said what's bugging Alex. She said Alex is getting more and more jumpy around you—all you give him these days are little grunts and commands, pretty soon he'll be actually hiding from you.

THURSDAY. Four hours sleep after two quarts of Coors and an unhappy twisting around in her bed. She announces to me at 4:30 A.M. that I'm trapped by my compulsive acquisitiveness—I never relinquish anything, people have to be pried away from me. I said look at the clock, can't it wait? She said Joe, you were whimpering something about Julie again in your sleep. I said look, I'm not responsible for what I say in my sleep, and I simply can't figure you out: for months you were badgering me to let you move in, so you finally moved in that whole miserable year in Capitola, and you turned sullen and swore I was smothering you, I was making it harder and harder to breathe, so then I forced you to pack up and leave and you got even worse, what in hell do you want! She said all right, get out of here, Joe, I'm so tired of this! I rolled over and went back to sleep.

TUESDAY. Sparrow is touchy again because I didn't drive down to his inner-space retreat at Pajaro Dunes. He mentioned that Adam Glockman had led a high-powered workshop on guilt. I said I'm sorry I missed that. He said no, you're not—you've never learned how to reach out: you've lived in all kinds of places with lovers and wives, but when you pull up your stakes it doesn't matter at all because you weren't really there, you just stand on the sidelines with your hands in your pockets and watch, there has never been a place that's been special to you.

Constanza showed up at my door very late with her attaché case and the dark circles under her eyes. She departed a few minutes ago, leaving me raw. She said boy, what a lover you've turned out to be. I said sweetheart, I'm not a machine. Even with the electrical prods I could feel the wind pushing us farther apart.

WEDNESDAY. Very low tide at Redwood City. Got caught in the mud near the mouth of the channel, the rudder fittings almost twisting off. A sudden strong puff: the boat eased over on its side, our oranges floating away. Waldo was scrambling frantically—he kept trying to dig his nails into the hull. Constanza yelled save him, you idiot, you know he can't swim!

I climbed up on the centerboard and got the boat righted. As I was trying to get him back into the cockpit Waldo snapped at my wrist. I cuffed the side of his nose. Constanza went into a rage: you son of a bitch, Joe, you exploit human beings, you're brutal to dumb animals! I told her to shut up, I was trying to get the boat moving again, but she kept pounding my chest with her fist, her face getting greenish, then practically white. I hauled in on the mainsheet as hard as I could, and the boat flipped us into the channel again. She didn't pound me the second time around.

THURSDAY. Rain. Spent an hour listening to Sparrow declaiming on creative procrastination in transpersonal relationships. I didn't get the connections he was trying to make. He said Joey, you didn't try.

Constanza insisted I get a tetanus shot for the bite. Now when I drive over to her cottage I sense ominous birds in the trees. She curls herself up in the big basket chair with her hash, the rum at her elbow and the dog in her lap. She keeps trying out her claws. She was using her claws when we shared the same roof, she is using her claws as we're drifting apart.

FRIDAY. Sparrow was unable to restrain himself at the

finance committee staff session this morning: motions and recommendations and qualifications and viable alternatives. I suggested during lunch that one circle of the Inferno be set aside for the finance committee freaks. Sparrow threw his fork down so hard that it bounced out of his plate. He said Joey, the only time I've seen you thaw out and be truly authentic is right after some woman has booted you out of her life—that's when you start rolling your eyes—but as soon as things stabilize you go back to the ice in your head. I said hey, am I really as bad as all that? He said worse.

MONDAY. Constanza appeared at my door around ten with her attaché case and the dog. After the third rum & Coke she was going nonstop like a disc jockey, her face changing colors again. I kept wondering how I could turn off the switch. She repeated her theory that I had willfully crippled myself because I couldn't get Julie to totally surrender to me—that's why I've become a lost cause in the sack. She was still crackling away at 2:30 A.M.

Awoke surly and raw. Drove to work, left instructions on the blackboard and crept to the faculty lounge. I was half-dozing on the cot in the side room when Sparrow discovered me and told me to get the hell out of the place, the palace guard would be coming down for coffee pretty soon and I was going to cut my own throat.

WEDNESDAY. Phoned Constanza to see if she had any rum. It was past midnight and she didn't want me to come. I drove over. She said look at your face, Jesus Christ, this is like Capitola all over again! I said do you remember how you kept complaining until I agreed you could move in with me, and then the complaints got much worse, and you couldn't even shoot any film, and you said I was digging a trench around you? She said I had very good reasons to complain and you know what they are—living with you, Joe, is like trying to pump up a tire full of holes.

Sparrow took me aside today and informed me he's going to lease a defunct Bible camp near Lake Tahoe and live on the grounds with his family and some friends and transform the place into a center for inner-space probes. He's asking a select few to invest their money and positive energy. I said Sparrow, I'm broke. He patted my shoulder and said well, I guess you are starting to pay for your sins.

TUESDAY. Watched impeachment maneuvering on the TV in the faculty lounge. Sparrow insists the impeachment was all orchestrated a long time ago. I said well, maybe so, but the steps are absorbing to watch anyway—Nixon looks like a character in a ballet executing a slow and meticulous dance to the edge of the cliff. Sparrow said Joey, that's so typical of you: you're obsessed with the way things conclude and decay.

Constanza asked if she could borrow my Master Charge card—Patrick writes he's discovering needs in himself only she can fulfill, so she may have to drive up and get him back on his feet. I said have a good time and threw the card in her lap. She said thanks. From the very beginning, I predicted it'd turn out like this.

III

Apr. 3, 1974–Apr. 21, 1974

WEDNESDAY. Constanza is mentally packing her bags. I lie next to her as she fingers the scar on her cheek and we hear the clock ticking. She said she was digging through some of the letters I had sent her last year, and except for the quotations from Rilke and Proust they sounded like some evangelist's admonitions to his dutiful wife. More hammering over the eyes from her terrible rum. This morning I leaned into the urinal that ricochets and walked up to the lectern to introduce John Stuart Mill with a couple of stains on the front of my pants.

SUNDAY. Sparrow explained to me that I never learned how

to express my psychic flow—he said you keep trying to dam up currents inside you that can't be contained. I said what do you want me to do? He said go with the flow. Dinner with Constanza. Her cousin had left some more of his deplorable hash. We were in bed before 11. In the middle of the night her phone jangles in my ear. She takes the phone into the bathroom. I stumble back into sleep.

THURSDAY. Constanza dug her nails into my shoulder and cried half the night. She said Joe, you equate love with slashing and pulling away. I said no, that's not true. She rammed her fist into the pillow and said I don't think you feel normal unless things are falling apart.

SUNDAY. Drove over to her cottage last night and almost turned around and came home. The purple chopper was parked out in front. I drove around the block a couple of times and then parked and went in. Constanza's cousin was clomping around in his boots making masculine utterances and popping beer cans. His latest girl friend had just kicked him out and he needed a place where he could crash for a while. She was feeding the turtles brine shrimp and watering the plants and studiously ignored me. The cats came and went. Waldo kept yawning and scratching himself. The kitchen got cluttered with wisecracks and flattened beer cans. He said he was working on a big Mexican deal—this could be really big. I asked him how big. He said awfully big. I left them smoking their hash on the front porch and drove back to the apartment. They were discussing the price of the hash. It was pretty good hash for a couple of indigents living at public expense.

MONDAY. Constanza complains she hasn't got enough strength of character to shake herself free, and she knows she can't keep sliding along like this, I am driving her into the ground with my long silences. I said what silences? She said

Joseph, you don't even know when you pull yourself into your shell. I said get rid of that cousin of yours and you'll see me emerge. She said my cousin has already moved out, and that isn't the trouble at all. I said how come you're always complaining?—the great lamentations seem to come from your side. She turned her back on me. I said Constanza, if you don't feel fulfilled you can always ring up your agent and shoot a few rolls of film instead of settling for food stamps and hash every night—just don't take out your tensions on me, you don't hear me complain. She said Joe, you're too devious to come out and complain but you've got your own ways of tormenting the people around you, there's a pretty good reference list.

SATURDAY. Departmental cioppino repast at Mandel's Friday night. The palace guard began their usual big scrutiny the moment Constanza appeared on my arm in her long Lady Dracula dress. She was smoking her little cigars. Mandel mentioned that I'd missed an awful lot of departmental sessions this year. I said I had over-extended myself, but I'd certainly try to be there the next time. He said okay, Joe, fine—have some wine.

Towards the end of the evening Sparrow put his arms around Constanza and me and led us out to the pool area. Sparrow's wife was dancing around in the den by herself. We were all pretty far gone. Sparrow clasped us to his bosom and assured Constanza with brimming eyes that he truly empathized with the anguish he saw in her face. He said you know, I've been watching this character here for quite a few years, and I love him like nobody else, except maybe my wife and my kids, he's like part of the family to me, but he's not to be trusted, Constanza, he is lethal to people who reach out to him—he holes up in his private little bunker until they start pulling away, then he rips himself open and spatters. I twisted away. Sparrow fell in the pool. I stumbled around the side of the house and got into the car and drove home.

IV

Apr. 26, 1974–May 28, 1974

FRIDAY. Constanza is jumpy. She says Patrick's presence has visited her several times recently, both inside the cottage and out in the yard. She makes her eyes large. Waldo has been whimpering and running in circles, and her car had a flat yesterday. This morning the toaster got stuck and shot sparks. I suggested she purchase some flash bulbs and get Patrick's penumbra on slides— Sparrow could use them for one of his Thursday night inner-space probes.

TUESDAY. She said she wanted to see Capitola again. Took another long walk along the tracks, Constanza carrying Waldo across the trestle in her arms. The river looked very low. A few ducks. Laughter from the Shadowbrook deck.

We strolled through the village. A new natural foods restaurant. The head shop had posters of Nixon & Gang behind bars. Waldo ran along the beach. The machinery kept grinding in me. She pressed her face against my shoulder and said she felt awful about all the walls that had come up between everyone, she had really tried to break through the walls. I said I didn't see why there had to be walls. She leaned into me and kept shaking her head. I said look, everything'll be fine. She said don't make me laugh.

SUNDAY. Woke up very early this morning feeling tremors of panic: something's got to be done! Made the necessary phone calls and transported the whole crew to San Juan Bautista, a crisp day, everyone cheerful and light, Constanza shooting several rolls of film in the mission cemetery, Laura spiriting Alex into the church for some kind of contrition exercise she'd cooked up in her head.

I stretched myself out in the middle of the grassy square and let the sun flutter over me. Alex stumbled out of the church with candle drippings all over his hands.

We stopped at the bakery for palm leaves and cheese and

ate lunch on the bleachers overlooking the rodeo ring. Constanza inserted her plastic Dracula fangs and lunged at our necks. Alex bit into her leg.

I took pictures of everyone, including the terrier, in the grape arbor behind the hotel. We walked over to the stables. When I lined them all up at the end of the bucket-brigade wagon, Constanza said hold it a second. She asked for the Pentax. I handed it to her. She flipped the back open, exposing the film. I grabbed the camera out of her hand. She said Joe, you're repeating your morbid rituals again! I said what are you talking about? She said go take a look at your famous collection of slides!

SATURDAY. Thirty-six nonstop hours of awareness exercises at Pajaro Dunes. The psychosynthesis facilitator showed up late looking drained: he'd been fighting freeway traffic all the way from Oakland. Sparrow pushed back the furniture as a skeletal woman in a flowing white gown was describing to me her accidental drowning in a pond in the winter of 1823. I asked how it happened. She said the ice broke and her cloak dragged her down—it had a lining of fur. I asked where was the pond. She said just outside Trenton, New Jersey.

The facilitator pulled off his shirt and we started our breathing. He explained about muscular control. I lay next to the woman in white. Her toes seemed strangely bent. I lost all track of time. We were moving from breathing to inner-space probes. The facilitator was asking us to walk down a flight of ten stairs. As I walked down the steps the woman in white began twisting my thumb. The facilitator said I want you to open the door that you see before you. I opened the door and stepped into a large empty room with a window. He said I want you to study whatever you see before you. I walked over to the window and looked out. The black water was rising, and the old skiff lay anchored a few yards away. He said go. As I climbed through the window and started to wade to the skiff I could feel my thumb aching. The woman was sucking on it. I pulled my hand back and got up from the floor and went out to the dunes.

The woman followed me out. She said hey, wait for me. I said go back inside. She said you're in a very bad space, aren't you. I said please go inside. She went back to the group. I stayed out on the dunes for a couple of hours.

WEDNESDAY. She's drifting again. Instead of checking with the agent for free-lance assignments she floats around the cottage over-feeding the turtles and drowning the plants while the terrier runs around sniffing Patrick's penumbra and squirting all over the floor. Then her cousin roars up on his bike and they light up a couple of joints and start slamming the wisecracks around. The cousin asks me to lend him a twenty, he's got an outrageous deal coming up. I inform him I don't have a twenty. He says okay, Joe, cool.

TUESDAY. I was going to lay off the rum but she had a fresh pint. We watched *Civilisation* and got into the hash. She kept rubbing her scar, so I knew things were happening upstairs. She was very affectionate and brought her electrical gadgets to bed. This morning she shook me awake. She said Joseph, I'm going away for a while. I said when. She said now.

V

May 31, 1974–Jun. 3, 1974

FRIDAY. Not a word. Awoke in the middle of the night—I was sure Waldo was scratching outside. I crawled out of bed. No Waldo. Got dressed and drove over to the cottage. I tried all the windows. The windows were locked. I sat on the stone bench in the back yard until I had smoked all my cigarettes, then drove home.

Half an hour after I went back to bed the phone rang: Claire was having more problems with the washing machine. I said listen, I'm not your repairman, it's been seven long years, would you kindly get off my back, all of you! She said goodness, Constanza has done it again, hasn't she? Click.

As I'm standing in the shower: is that the phone? As I'm walking to the car: is that the phone?

SUNDAY. Every time I called Julie the architects claimed she was out in the field, but I drove past her office and saw her car parked in the usual slot. When I tried reaching her at home I kept getting busy signals. I had almost forgotten the barbed wire she erects.

When I told Sparrow about Constanza's flight up to Portland he said what did you expect, Joe— you knew the first week you took up with that woman it'd happen this way, you even gave me the entire scenario—and for Christ's sake leave Julie alone! I said Sparrow, I've always left Julie alone. He said Joey, you're impossible, you don't understand how relationships work: fourteen years I've been married, three sons who play soccer, a house in Los Altos I practically built by myself, including the wiring, a wife who sings Bach cantatas and goes jogging with me every morning at six—that's stability, Joe, that is growth, and that kind of stability you simply can't handle, it scares you away—at least you could have the common decency to leave your ex-wives alone, especially considering how you set them all up and then walked out on them. I said I never set anyone up, and I never walked out on anyone. Sparrow said have it your own way and left.

To Bolinas yesterday, Laura and Alex leaping into the surf in their jeans. I watched a couple of very young girls riding bareback across the wet pebbles and shells. The fog burned off by noon and the sun struck the Tamalpais hills.

We had fruit balls and organic root beer at the Full Earth. I remembered the cook—he had worked at the North Side cantina when I was living in Berkeley with Claire and finishing graduate school. I asked Laura if she remembered the old days in Berkeley—she couldn't have been more than three. She said no.

The Full Earth waitress was hostile: too many outsiders

descending upon Bolinas these days, pretty soon it'll be like Carmel. She said she had come to Bolinas from Stockton because she had heard it was rustic and quiet, but if things got much worse she was going to split up to Humboldt County or some place like that. Alex said the organic root beer tasted like ink. I kept brooding over Constanza. The hammering returned every time I remembered she still had my Master Charge card. Laura kept glancing at me. She kept her mouth shut but seemed pleased.

MONDAY. If she knocked on my door in the middle of the night with the terrier in her arms I would send her away, yet I keep waiting for that knock. I want to find some way of making her sting. She had kept me off-balance for over two years with her damned petulance, always demanding what I didn't possess or what I couldn't give up, taunting me that I hadn't been able to forget everything that had happened to me. I don't know when we first started sliding apart. Months ago, when I asked her to pack up her things and clear out of the bungalow in Capitola, she said Joseph, you'd better stop looking for closeness and warmth, it does bad things to you. I said please get your things out of here. We had been sailing that day and the sails lay bunched up on the floor. She looked at the sails and the couch and the photographs tacked to the wall and said all terminations begin in the mind and walked out.

The Indians Don't Need Me Any More

1

I suppose that was it: the last of my Alcatraz runs. I won't be hauling any more clothing and food to the entrenched Indians. It's a series of very long tacks from the Palo Alto yacht harbor to the Rock—a whole day's trip when the winds aren't good—and I finally had to admit as I was tying the *Wanderer* up the last time that I'm not really helping the American Indian Movement all that much with the few boxes of blankets and canned goods I've been able to buy or collect around here. Legal aid would be better, along with some solid political support. Ritchie wants a big generator. *There's the psychology to think about, too.* They've got enough blankets and Spam. And now that Nancy has finally remarried, and it's clear that my contract will not be renewed at Peninsula State, I'm ready to clean out my cottage, get rid of the hookah and the scented drip candles, and try again some other place.

I used to think all those shuttles in the sloop were a sign of my altruism at work. Social concern. But the truth is I found a great solace in watching the winds and the tides when I first started sailing last summer. Handling a tiller was good therapy, it kept my body and mind occupied and took me away from the traps I had set for myself. And having a meaningful destination made my hours on the water more rich—it was more than just sliding around. When I looked at the hull of the boat the other day I could see it's absorbed a real beating from the northwesterly winds. I'll have to unload it even though it's a bad time to sell. I can't afford it any more.

I'm going to start packing. Roll up that Harpo Marx poster tacked over my desk. That grin has been getting on my nerves. And there's something else telling me it's time to stop licking the wounds. Once again I can feel the machinery about to start grinding in me. Sparrow noticed it, too: he said I look as if I'm about to lock myself into a different position. Since the children have finally accepted their new Field & Stream dad, who will give them the discipline and care they both need and deserve, I might as well get on my feet. I've used up the bay.

2

As I was sailing away from the Indians today I had to finally admit that the life I've been trying to hammer together has left me empty and raw. I hadn't expected that. *Fulfillment* and *actualization* seemed easy enough to wrap up and take home when I had Abraham Maslow on the lectern before me, reinforced by my neatly-typed notes and the formulas clearly outlined on the board. Even the pointer I swung back and forth felt authentic.

As the *Wanderer* was sailing under the Bay Bridge I found myself staring straight up at the massive steel girders, and that brought back the feel of the rigid geometry that would press against me at Peninsula State—in the classrooms, in the faculty lounge, even down by the tennis courts—and that little flash took me back to the Friday last May when I lost my cool while doing Tolstoy. Everything seemed to be pushing against me that Friday. Even the sidewalks on campus were slamming up needlessly hard against my arches. Off and on, over a period of several months, I'd been trying for one final clarification between Nancy and me, despite this new IBM man in her life who happened to hit it off beautifully with the kids, and for a short while we seemed to have worked up an actual glow between us, with the widower temporarily on the sidelines, but already I could sense the glow dying, since nothing was happening, we couldn't really change the deep core of whatever we were. *No good, no good,* I kept thinking, remembering the glow that was starting to spread out to Laura and Alex, *already they're lightening up, not nearly so tense, no longer crying at night, but it isn't going to work, and this glow in the children is a terrible thing to see.* I had just had them over for the weekend: the zoo, Marine World, rattling cable cars out to Fisherman's Wharf, just the three of us having a ball, no apprehensive Mom snapping *Alex needs his nap!,* no griping about garbage sacks or the dog's bone on the couch—and then *wham!* as I was walking across campus and thinking back to that marvelous weekend, I found myself aching for leaves to rake, weeds to yank out of the ground, dirty dishes to wash, someone else flushing the toilet, the sounds of can openers, the slamming of doors. I was also hung over. The night before, loaded on sherry, I had driven down Hopkins Street with the headlights off. Craig's 4-wheel drive Toyota was parked in my former driveway, and all the curtains were drawn in the house. I kept reminding myself as I drove back to the cottage not to let this sort of thing happen again.

3

It was a hot Friday. I was sweating so hard in my bush jacket and turtleneck jersey that I finally wadded a couple of paper towels under my armpits, but the towels got soggy and slid down the sleeves. Sparrow and my other colleagues were ambling from class to class in their usual short-sleeved drip-dry shirts like NASA engineers, but I stuck to the turtleneck and boots I'd decided would best represent the real me, plus the other bold touches designed to impress and seduce undergrads—the torn jeans and the shades. That was part of the contract, I figured, getting the Camaro crowd turned on to Yeats and Flaubert using all the theatricals at your command, including the proper cosmetics. You had to relate.

By the time my 2 P.M. class had dragged around that Friday I could feel the bad ache in my shoulders and neck. Every time I thought back to the split in my life, and the way it was bruising the kids, I would start to concoct weekend jaunts in my mind—Mendocino, Carmel, the whole family packed into the Hillman convertible along with a fictitious sheep dog I would throw in to finish the scene (Jip wasn't quite right for the part) like a Standard Oil billboard. But I could never imagine us alone, just Nancy and me. Not comfortably. Too much distance had crystallized between us, and it wouldn't thaw out. I couldn't imagine myself totally alone with her, the two of us seated at a restaurant table, a couple of menus and an ashtray between us, and this was peculiar because I know I felt jealousy and remorse, especially after Craig started coming around. It grated against me, and yet it was clear I would have to accept the brute fact that those crystals were permanently there. So would she. Shortly before moving into the cottage, I had told her, *You won't accept this until later, but the truth is you'll get nothing good out of me until after we've split. You're still young—you deserve a fresh start.*

As I walked into class I could spot a real bummer in the making. Their eyes told me, the tilt of their frames. I pushed them through ten, fifteen minutes of the Tolstoy, clutching my chest, acting out Ivan Ilyich's torment and death, everything but the actual screaming, but when I finally finished my performance they responded with a silence so solid and compressed you could haul it away in a furniture van.

I leaned against the desk: artificial pearls cast out to genuine swine. "So what's he saying—*Ivan Ilyich's life had been most simple and most ordinary, and therefore most terrible*—what does that mean?"

Their eyeballs were barely twitching. I waited. Nothing. I could see Sparrow standing outside, as though checking me out. George McManus was meditating on his thumb. A girl yawned.

I threw my stuff into the briefcase. *Zap:* there was the Toyota again, parked directly behind Nancy's green

Maverick. "You're really disgusting," I said quietly and walked out, leaving them sitting there with their plywood expressions. I went to my car. *They haven't learned how to decipher the plain printed page!* I was feeling so bad I left tracks. I could hear Sparrow yelling to me. I ignored him. I had heard it all before.

The faculty lot seemed to be buckling with heat. I left the Menlo Park campus by way of El Camino Real and winced all the way into Palo Alto, the sun rubbing my eyes like a file. As soon as I approached my own turf I felt better. The tree-lined avenues felt cool, almost damp, and the elegantly decaying old houses dating back to the '80s and '90s, with their towers and panes of stained glass, the verandas and warped picket fences, were comforting: a world decomposing, waiting for the bulldozers, a dark falling-apart, a rich calm. Rows of diseased palm trees. Cast-iron sprinklers revolving on the lawns. I drove up to my cottage holding my breath. I listened: no motorcycles, no rock and roll. I relaxed.

4

The little place I'd been renting the last couple of years sat directly in back of a once-magnificent estate dating back to the founding of Stanford University. Since the end of the Korean War the big house had been gerrymandered into several small units, but the owners, an elderly couple in Burlingame, were merely sitting on the property, waiting and watching the land values climb, and so they had let the old mansion with its thick, crazy hedges and fruit trees disintegrate, one window and board at a time. When I moved into the cottage the week Nancy filed for divorce, the last of the tenants, a bachelor accountant who kept plants in his room, was in the process of moving out. *It's impossible,* he confided to me as he hauled out his flowerpots, *the plumbing doesn't work. Take a look at the roof.* The roof was full of bare patches where the shingles had come off.

So for several months the Victorian relic stood empty and

dark. It was balm for my soul. I had my secluded retreat less than ten blocks away from my previous home, and Laura was able to drop by after school to visit with me whenever she felt like it. *This is your cottage, you know,* I assured her. *Most kids have only one home, you've got two, how about that. Huh?* She came around fairly often, especially at first, because she thought it was all kind of neat, but sometimes the whole situation confused her, and she'd squint at the light-blue light bulbs with the Tiffany shades, and the candles, and the hookah that set me back sixty-five bucks, and the posters of Harpo and W. C. Fields, and ask, *Dad, how come you're living like a teenager?*

But I had the lush, untended gardens all to myself, with the pigeons working their wings like propellers in the palms, and the lime trees and bougainvillea, the secluded green circles of clover and moss where I'd stretch out after work and accept the sun into my pores, Ravel drifting out of my windows like smoke. I was suffering over Nancy, of course, and over the other women who were plowing themselves through my life, creating the usual gouges and cuts. They came and they went, but invariably they came on too strong, leaving their toothbrushes, badgering me over the phone late at night, and I wasn't ready for any of that, not with my old world still heavy on my mind. I fixed the young ladies nice beef stroganoffs and bought a good water bed, but they didn't know when to quit. And the aching slid forward and back in my chest.

5

Then the free spirits moved in.

I was fixing my chicken and rice one tranquil afternoon, Casadesus filling the cottage with *Le tombeau de Couperin,* when a couple of young men in bib overalls loped into the kitchen. Could they borrow my john? They had taken out a lease on the big house and found all the toilets clogged. They used my bathroom, phoned the plumber, and went out to their VW bus. Ten minutes later they were back at my door.

Got any boards around here?

Boards?

Boards. Planks. That front lawn is awfully damp.

I went out with them. They had backed their bus, which was loaded with mattresses and food, up to the front door, and the wheels had sunk in on either side of the cement walk. I looked at the furrows gouged out by the spinning rear wheels.

I haven't got any planks.

The taller of the two pulled a rubber band from his wrist and grabbed the back of his mane and twisted it. He slipped the rubber band on. *Might as well unload. Want to give us a hand?*

I spent the next couple of hours hauling in pots and pans, sacks of flour and rice, boxes of canned goods, and of course the mattresses.

You've sure got a lot of mattresses.

Yeah.

That night I slept my best sleep in weeks, no moaning, no dreams, and I awoke the next morning with my arms aching but my head very bright. I hadn't had a single slug of sherry before hitting the sack, and it felt novel and good to wake up with a clean skull and all the headpieces fitting into place. When I glanced out the window I saw, in addition to the VW bus, a converted milk truck and an Easy Rider bike. I went outside. The milk truck had Oregon plates and was coated with dust.

When I came home from the campus that night a strange Studebaker pickup, outfitted with a wooden camper complete with a stovepipe and a kerosene lantern hanging from the doorknob, was occupying my stall in the carport, and now there were two motorcycles on the lawn. The rear wheel was off on one of the choppers, and a pockmarked kid wearing a floppy leather hat with a turkey feather was working on the chain. I parked my Hillman in the street and walked over. He glanced at me.

You happen to have a torque wrench?

No.

He resumed his tinkering.

Do you know who belongs to that truck?

What truck?

That Studebaker in the carport.

He shook his head. *Nope.*

6

Troubled in spirit, I went into the cottage, and while I was trying to grade a few papers before supper—*The Celebration of the Dionysian Principle in Hesse*—I could hear yet another set of pistons roar up to the front of the house, and then voices, this time the laughter of skinny girls, *Oh wow, out of sight!* and then an electric guitar started blatching out chord after chord from one of the rear dormer windows of the big house—no progression, no melody, just a blatching of random chords. I got up and closed all my windows.

Well. I thought about it. They were, after all, leasing the place and its grounds for hard cash, and were therefore entitled to run their commune any way they saw fit. And besides, they were healthy and young and conditioned to live in a world full of amplification and pounding exhausts.

The week before, I had just finished doing *Gatsby* at school, and it struck me just then that there were some connections between that Fitzgerald milieu—all those parties and motor excursions and teas—and the blatching of the electric guitar. I flashed myself back to my twenties and late teens, to the boarding house in New Haven where the volleyball boys raised the same banal hell every day and got predictably smashed on a few cans of beer every alternate night, and then to my basement cubicle on Chicago's North Side, where there wasn't fresh air and my only companion was an elderly muscatel freak who had lost control over his bladder, and then to the long, lonely rides on the El to my classes in Jackson Park, the solitary meals and the stark cafeterias with tiled floors and walls and all the menial jobs, one after the other, as I worked my way through the first years of graduate school, before Nancy showed up. And then I realized I was biting my lip over the free spirits in their kibbutz because I had never had anything like the contact they'd worked out for themselves, creating a network of interests in some ways not really so different from Scott Fitzgerald's golf games and midwinter proms. Faces and places and names. At their age—at the age of nineteen or twenty I'd be walking along Lake Michigan completely alone, my brain turning inward as usual, absorbed in its own processes, my loneliness following my tracks like a dog, just the surf of the lake on one side and the whine of the Outer Drive traffic on the other. The Beatles hadn't been invented. Acapulco gold didn't exist. Small wonder I found such a refuge in Nancy the moment she came on the scene in my Age of Johnson class, and that I dug into her like a clamp for eleven long years. And this explained, possibly, why I found the spontaneous gregariousness in the big house, along with the noises it brought, so unsettling. The free spirits made me think of the volleyball boys in New Haven, and the tiled cafeterias, and the muscatel freak.

7

But at any rate, the big house was silent that Friday. No blatches, no bikes. Two mongrels were lying on their sides in the middle of the alley, paws stretched out stiff, like freeway fatalities. I circled around them and parked and went into my place. I had ceased troubling my head over the portable kiln someone had tilted on its side in the bed of primroses and then apparently abandoned, or the overstuffed chair with the cigarette burns sitting under the pomegranate tree, or the empty wine jugs on the porch, the deer skulls propped up on the fence. They were simply a part of my life, like the smog hanging over the Santa Clara valley, the decanter of sherry on my desk. My folders and notes were jammed into the briefcase like wallpaper samples I was being paid to hustle. They had little connection with the slippery feel of the children as they sat face to face in the tub, my hands soaping their necks, or with the strained mouth of their mother those feverish early months when I wasn't quite sure where I'd be sleeping that night, and her whispers as we sat side by side on the steps of the back porch, the kids watching cartoons on TV, *What do you need that you can't get from me?* and her sudden stiffening as my fingers touched her elbow.

I stared out the door of the cottage. The unexpected silence had caught me off guard. My mind started picking through past memories the way a pick probes for fragments of food. I sat down at my desk. Harpo was grinning at me. My journal was lying on top of a stack of term papers, like a press. I opened it at random—any entry would do. This one went back a few years, to the period when everything was presumably still intact:

> *April 12, 1966. Again the chloroform on the tongue, nothing working between us, the rooms of the house like compartments for storing up silence. We poke at our dinner and strain to concoct dialogue, but the forks make more noise. Strangers at least have perfunctory exchange, a few ceremonial nods. Sparrow says I look terrible again. All evening I found myself hassling Laura about her Mary Poppins record, TURN IT DOWN! TURN IT DOWN! and finally I gave her a crack across the rear that set her spinning. I'd like to understand my machinery better, figure out what exactly is freezing me up and then making me boil. Poor design. Everybody gets caught. Mean irritations and lust.*

8

I heard a motorcycle drive up to the big house, then the VW bus. A bird started beating its wings inside me. I had papers to grade, work to do. Now the camper, horn honking. I slammed shut my journal and stuck it up on the shelf.

In the past, when the pressures built up, I could always

drop over at Nancy's, have a cup of Sanka and play with the children and Jip for a while. Mow the lawn. Following the divorce we became tolerable friends, almost close, since we finally had something in common, and there were nights when I tortured myself over her. When I wasn't entertaining some woman, I kept pictures of Nancy on my desk. And then suddenly, before I was ready for him, her IBM admirer showed up and declared Nan off limits to me. Suddenly it was no longer possible to cruise over to Hopkins Street and ring the doorbell whenever I felt the need for that bell. I guess I had figured on keeping the whole business on ice over there, tucked away for emergency use. She finally had everything that I wanted for her, and it hurt.

I fixed myself a pan of tuna and noodles. *Forge on!* I kept telling myself. After dinner I started grading the papers, the decanter at my side. When I finished the sherry around ten I got into the car and drove to the Green Goose. I stayed there for a couple of hours.

Then I remember it's raining, but lightly, and I'm driving down Hopkins Street with my lights off, and there's that Toyota again in the driveway, and the windows are dark. I drive on, down Middlefield Avenue, and I turn up some side street and notice I can't get the wipers to work, although I keep twisting the knob back and forth, and then I feel a peculiar bump which I can't account for, and suddenly I'm chugging in second gear not on the street but up the manicured lawn of the Wesleyan Methodist Church, unable to stop, my foot sliding off the clutch pedal, and then I notice the windshield's got cracks in a number of places, and I get the car back on the street and somehow manage to navigate it home.

The next morning, when I finally struggled to get out of bed and go out to the carport, and when I saw how the front end had been flattened by some incredible flattening machine, I simply turned around and crawled back to bed. I didn't know what I'd hit. I didn't want to find out. The questions didn't come until several days later. I should've known better, of course, and reported it at once. Sparrow says the delay cost me my job. Yesterday he said, *Go join the Indians up there on the Rock*.

9

It isn't clear what exactly is happening on Alcatraz. Sparrow claims they are going to dig in permanently. *Time* says in its cover story: GOODBYE TO TONTO. It's obvious that the kind of relief they've been getting will have to give way to something more substantial. Ritchie is right. He poured me a cup of coffee from his thermos today and said, "Send us a couple of good electricians. And a big generator."

He was looking at me strangely—he seemed almost embarrassed. A Coast Guard cutter was idling a few hundred yards away. It hurt me a little to hear Ritchie talk like that, after all the heavy seas I had plowed the *Wanderer* through, and he must have noticed, because he said, "Look, you've done a great job. Everybody has done a great job." Then he leaned forward. "Mind if I say something?"

"What?" The coffee was sloshing out of the cup.

"Aren't you pushing yourself a bit hard?"

I stared at him.

He gave me the same kind of look I would sometimes lay on my students. "The first time I saw you ram that little boat into the dock I said, *Jesus, now here is one wild character!* You remember?"

I laughed. Then I saw his expression. "What is it, Ritch?"

The boom was beginning to swing. Ritchie grabbed it. "Don't get me wrong. I'm not trying—." He shifted his weight. "You don't look very healthy."

"I feel fine."

"Look, it isn't my business, but you really look bad and it's bothering me. The others have noticed it, too. We don't want anyone jeopardizing their health. You look worse every time you come out. How much weight have you lost, anyway? That's an awfully long trip you've been making in the boat—it'd be a lot simpler to haul the stuff up to the city in your car. Drop it off at the Center. I mean you know we appreciate every sack of potatoes we get, but—you really look bad. You look like you've lost—."

"Okay, Ritchie." I handed him the cup. "You're probably right."

"It's senseless to burn yourself out. We're not hurting that bad."

"Okay, Ritch."

He kept holding the boom so it wouldn't swing out. "It's time we got moving on something more solid." He backed away. "Like a big generator. There's the psychology to think about, too."

"All right, Ritch."

As I pushed the sloop off he saluted me by shaking his fist. The sails luffed and snapped, suddenly filled with wind. I shook my fist back, but I could see that the Indians don't need me any more.

The Afterglow of Decay

I: 1956

—The bluff in back of Kurt's house in Santa Monica has eroded by almost six feet. When I sit in the kitchen with Mother I can hear the surf grinding away. Claire noticed more cracks in the foundation, and I told Kurt that the floors are beginning to tilt, but he assured us that the old place would be good for another thirty years and dismissed the erosion as a natural feature of the Southern California seashore. His hair is turning gray and I noticed new lines in his face and a new restlessness.

For a few minutes after we arrived Mother couldn't remember Claire's name. She received her with cautious politeness, as though she were meeting her daughter-in-law for the first time. She's shrivelled a lot in the last couple of years and is starting to look almost hollow, but she was in good spirits and meandered again, pretty much like the last time, about the remarkable years when the family band was on tour, the debates in the front of the bus, the rehearsals in church basements, in Scandinavian fields, the fine sailor outfits that Anna and Britt made for me, how I captured the heart of the audience night after night as I marched out on the stage and made my smart little bow with the baton in my hand, and the time we had left Franz by mistake in the Estonian village—there had been a fierce snowstorm. And then her thoughts shifted to Father's great winter in Danzig the year I was born, and to the glorious breakthrough that spirit-filled August in Prague, and the hush when he ascended into the pulpit, all those hungering souls caught and held by his eyes. She read us a portion of his most recent letter:

The Enemy Voices have finally forced me to give up the fight in the Brazilian jungles, and the Master has directed my steps to the Peruvian frontier. There will be soul-winning campaigns, etc. She stopped reading and folded the letter and said the rest is instructions and personal thoughts. I said well, so he's off to Peru. Kurt turned on me sharply. He said Joseph, you have never understood the significance of that man.

That evening, after dinner, Claire and I went to the bookstore with him. It was even more chaotic than the last time, the shelves in disorder, books on chairs, books on the floor, more than half of the lightbulbs burned out. I said shouldn't you get this place straightened out? He said don't talk like a janitor.

He was showing me two new "provocative" studies of Tillich and Bultmann when I noticed that Claire had slipped into the Intimate Literature room. I felt embarrassed for Kurt and maneuvered him up to the front of the shop and asked questions about Rudolf Bultmann, and when she finally came out she was silent and flushed. Later that night, as I was falling asleep, she dug her nails into my back and said Kurt is a terrible man.

—*Winter. Mother stops rocking. I can feel her hand patting my back. Father stands in the doorway. No words. The cat stares from the bed. When he walks down the stairs she starts rocking again. Kurt comes into the room and the cat disappears.*

—Mother still lowers herself down the rickety stairs to the beach every day, even when there is fog, with her Thomas à Kempis and her binoculars. She said Kurt gives me great comfort these days, he comes home from the bookstore and we have our devotional hour and I feed him his favorite soups.

The second night we were here he drove us in his dented Cadillac to a faith-healing extravaganza in downtown L.A. Cancerous tissue was neutralized and dental cavities were filled by the power of the Word. Kurt was overcome and wept several times. After the spiritual festival he bought us Singapore slings at the Hollywood Tiki Hut, a good place for fellowship and reflection. He became very restless and tried putting through a phone call. Framed by torches and Polynesian masks, his face changed its color and shape. He asked the cocktail waitress if the Indonesian girls had been in. She said no. Kurt ordered a fresh round of Singapore slings and confessed he was having fresh struggles with the flesh—twin sisters this time, Indonesian and highly gifted but possibly insincere. He had met them at the Tiki Hut one night and was struck by their spiritual potential and had gone home with them to exchange loving closeness, but they borrowed some money the following week and he hadn't seen them since. I asked how much money. He said the amount isn't important, don't think like an accountant.

He stared into his drink and said what have you heard about Franz? I said only that Franz is still hiding somewhere in New York—he has left his third wife and is trying to finish a book. Kurt said the Quaile family has been damaged beyond belief by its mania for false aspirations and Franz is the worst of the lot, let's get out of this place with these heathenish masks.

—The ships creak in the harbor and a horse passes us, nostrils steaming, its hooves striking the wet cobblestones. Franz looks frightened. The wheels of the lumbering wagon make a terrible noise. Kurt glares at a man on a bicycle who has stopped and is staring at us. I back myself into Mother's thick coat.

—Christmas Eve we took Mother to a candlelight service at the Full Bible Church in Long Beach. Claire seemed happy and kept pressing herself against my arm. Through most of the service Kurt kept his eyes closed and he seemed to be muttering to himself. Whenever the singing began Mother jumped to her feet, but I noticed she sang different songs. After the candlelight service Kurt became very restless again. He bought us hot chocolate and pie at a Sambo's and sat playing with his fork while we finished our pies. He said Joseph, you should pay more attention to your wife. Claire laughed. On the way back to Santa Monica he drove through several red lights. Mother said please, darling, you're going too fast. He ignored her. He dropped us off and drove away. Mother said Kurt spends many nights unpacking books in the shop until dawn.

He returned around noon the next day. He looked ravaged and said he was hungry. As Mother was fixing his bacon and eggs he rapped on the kitchen table and said let's get down on our knees and submit to the King. Mother shut off the gas burner and we knelt as he prayed for our souls.

—The marketplace is throbbing with voices and smells. Eels lie slithering in wooden handcarts. Franz is poking at chickens in crates. An old woman thrusts a live eel in my face. I start crying as Kurt pulls me away. The old woman laughs with black teeth.

—Kurt asked me this morning if I'd gotten any closer to finding my calling. I said no, I'm still looking around. He said Joseph, you're floundering again, your philosophy books have been false advocates—and don't listen to Franz with his literary pretensions, only after you give up your hollow vanities will you know what to do. Mother gave him a kiss and said Kurt has become very wise. Later he took me aside and said be more attentive to Claire, she gets easily bruised, can't you see the pained look in her eyes? I said when did you turn yourself into an expert on married life? He said I'm not talking about married life, I am talking about someone's soul. Then he lowered his voice and said you are still riddled with pride.

II: 1957

—Father phoned from the San Francisco airport minutes after I'd gone out on the route. Claire picked me up and we drove back to the post office and Battson went in as relief. We drove down to the airport at once.

He was dozing in the main terminal with his single

suitcase, beard untrimmed, a stench coming out of his clothes. He didn't recognize me: it had been almost ten years. He said the vomiting began in San Juan, a nagging stomach disorder. He was on his way to draw strength from Mother's porridge and Kurt's prayers when the sickness got worse and he had to get off the plane.

Claire went to the airport dispensary while I sat in the terminal with him. He said let us go to your house. In a minute, I said. He said you are blessed with a very fine wife, I can see the devotion in her eyes. I said yes. He asked what I was doing these days. I explained I was working as a postman across the bay in Sausalito. I didn't mention my unpublished manuscripts. He said service is paramount, the most honorable thing we can do with our gifts is to learn how to serve, never mind the rewards, there is no higher calling than this. I told him to rest. He wiped his mouth on his sleeve and said son, I praise God when I think how you boys have turned out. I kept wondering what had happened to Claire. I said isn't it tiring to travel so much at your age? You've been wandering for so many years, won't you settle down now? He looked at his suitcase and said we must go where the Master directs. Claire came back. The doctor was waiting for us in the dispensary.

Father kept pushing the stethoscope away—he insisted that this was quite needless, he'd continue his journey after spending a restful night under our roof. The doctor looked at his watch.

We followed the ambulance to the hospital in San Mateo and seven hours later the doctor announced he was dead. I asked what it was. He said wait for the autopsy, please. The nurse came. They had put a railing around his bed but he had clambered out over the railing and was roaming down the hall asking people for paper and pen when he finally fell. I phoned Kurt. He was silent at first, then became animated, as though he had just won a point.

—I try to sit quietly next to Franz as Father leans forward in the pulpit and points to the doors at the back of the church: there is something he wants everybody to do. Mother stares straight ahead. The choir sings about the blood of the lamb.

Suddenly I'm awake, the house dark, rectangles of light on the ceiling. Father is in his nightshirt, pacing, pacing. He will break through the walls. Franz is turning around in his sleep. Long after Mother stops crying the pacing goes on.

The asylum is surrounded by a high wooden wall. Franz has climbed up the telephone pole but won't tell me what's happening inside. Anna takes my hand: I must never try to peek through the knotholes because the lunatics crouch on the other side of the wall and poke out people's eyes with pencils and sticks. They sit for hours like that, locked away from the rest of the world, quietly waiting for somebody's eyes. I ask what's an asylum. Kurt appears and explains that an asylum is a prison for unsteady minds.

—Max showed up first with a black mourning band and a briefcase full of newspaper clippings of his most recent musical triumphs. When Mother and Kurt arrived her first comment to me was dear Joseph, have the herring come in? Anna and Britt brought their husbands and wept. Finally we were all together, except of course Franz—no one knew where he was, but they agreed he was doing the family no good with his scathing short stories which kept twisting the truth.

Kurt delivered an impromptu eulogy: Father had heard the command and obeyed to the ultimate hour, he had fought the significant fight and had died with the banner of the King in his hand. Mother nodded and gave me a wink.

The old family myths were dragged out, and I sat in the corner and watched as they compared the dimensions of their souls. Ancient betrayals materialized one more time. Kurt remembered how Franz had wantonly broken his pencils just before we arrived in the States. Little arguments flared up:

how to dispose of Father's personal effects, what to do with his papers, who would take custody of the trunk where he stored all his journals and manuscripts. He had left behind no savings and no bank account.

After Mother lay down for her nap they discussed her support. There was some haggling over quotas and ability to pay. Kurt opened a fresh pint of Scotch and announced that Mother would continue to remain under his protection and care in Santa Monica. Britt objected: he was hardly a suitable guardian for her, the poor woman shouldn't be forced to endure his warped world full of sexual demons and perverted women, to say nothing of all that unmentionable lewdness he peddled in the back of his shop. Mother awoke and said children, it's time for our tea. Anna slapped Kurt and received a sharp blow on the ear. Kurt grabbed Mother and left in the old Cadillac. Anna screamed stop him! he's kidnapping her!

—I pull the drawer open and discover the remains of two rats. Smears of blood on the white handkerchiefs. I close the drawer and go back downstairs. Father is loping from room to room, as though searching for something that's hidden somewhere. Mother stands in the kitchen, her hand on the edge of the stove. The door slams. Through the window I see Father between the pear trees.

III: 1960

—Kurt came clanking down the road Friday afternoon and stayed for the weekend. He had thrown Mother's two jars of borscht into the trunk of the car, along with a stuffed alligator for Laura. I had to wash the trunk out with the hose. He looked around at the West Marin hills, covered with sheep, and at the Point Reyes peninsula off in the distance, and said breathe in this air, Joseph, what a God-given retreat, this is where you will be purified! Claire broiled the four quail I had shot. After dinner we sat on the porch of the ranch house and talked. Kurt said listen to the sheep in the hills!

The next morning we took the .22 and hiked down to the

abandoned cabin at the edge of the glen. Claire stayed home with Laura—she said every time that man comes around I start getting depressed. Kurt described the new darkness that had settled upon him the last time he had visited Father's grave, and the sudden resurgence of his demons, full force, this time through a Ukrainian Baptist with unorthodox appetites. He unbuttoned his shirt: there were welts on his shoulder and back. I said Kurt, I don't understand you. He said Joseph, the Lord gives us difficult paths and we go.

As we were approaching the cabin he announced he could see something ominous building up in my life. Claire has certainly gotten more haggard and withdrawn—and she used to be so happy and light. I said it's just the adjustment to the isolation of this ranch. He said no, I predict that the silence between you will only increase, you had no business marrying her, and on top of that now there's the child. I said how can you lecture me, Kurt, with those welts on your back? He said Joseph, I see what I see. He stopped suddenly and pried the Winchester out of my hands. A fawn was staring at us less than thirty feet away. Kurt said we will have venison for dinner tonight. I said no, it's against the law. He said the law is suspended *a fortiori* when subsistence is at stake, and cut loose with a couple of shots that went into the brush. The fawn disappeared. He gave me the rifle and grumbled that the sights weren't properly aligned.

That evening he took us to the Union Hotel in Occidental for dinner. An elderly Italian was playing an accordion in the bar. Kurt talked earnestly about the Ukrainian Baptist—how the Lord uses her as a goad and a scourge. Every time they engage in some new beastliness, there is fresh devastation and then the inexpressible joy of rebirth. I said what makes you think that the Lord is involved in your sexual escapades? He said Joseph, the Spirit appears in circuitous ways, and attacked the spaghetti as though there were crawling things in the sauce.

I couldn't get to sleep the last night he was here. He kept walking through the ranch house, back and forth. I could hear him in the hired man's room, evidently poring over my notes for the latest manuscript. He went out to his Cadillac and sat listening to the radio for a while, twirling the dial constantly. He was coughing his alcohol cough. Early this morning, just before he drove off, he kissed Laura, then held us and groaned. He said you will always be stained until you plunge yourself into the blood of the lamb.

—Father will not be with us for Christmas again. The Lord has revealed there is work to be done in the Baltic outposts, and the need is severe. Kurt is starting to help Mother manage the family affairs. He says let's organize a family band. Franz is learning the clarinet. I lie back on the cushion in his room as he works on the fingering, a ferocity in his eyes.

—Phone call from Kurt: I have reliable information from Max that Franz is at work with diabolical intensity on an outrageous satire of Father and the family band—what an irony, since Franz with his lifelong withdrawal and heart full of doubts is the last person in the world to have anything reliable to say about Father's great ministry or the family's accomplishments. We will have to watch him with a vigilant eye, there could be mischief there. Father wore out his heart in the service of the King and I will not permit sarcasm or sneers. And now Mother is slipping and has to be helped to the beach.

—Kurt drove up for the Thanksgiving rabbit and quail I had shot. He asked what's this meat? I said pieces of young venison. He said yes, I can feel the wild strength in the flesh. No further talk about Franz. He said Mother is getting much worse and it's almost impossible to take her anywhere because she forgets about her bodily functions and has accidents. Claire said she needs a good nurse. He said the Spirit is watching over her.

He kept talking about the Spirit. The Spirit is with him again, keeping watch. The Ukrainian Baptist contracted venereal disease and went back to her husband in Toledo, Ohio. Later, when we were alone, he declared I should cease forcing my daughter and wife to exist like pariahs just because I have private vanities I wish to pursue, it's not good for the child. I said nobody's getting forced to do anything around here, and I don't see how you're in any position to talk with your demons and seamy affairs, but he didn't let up and he didn't seem to hear. Finally I stopped listening and went out of the house with the dog.

Friday we drove to the Russian River and he rented a canoe. Laura played on the beach. Claire took the canoe and paddled upstream by herself for a couple of hours. Kurt asked if I'd heard further news about Franz's distorted experiment in prose. I said no—how do you know it's distorted? He said I know it's distorted because I've examined his heart.

—*The man in the boat works says get out of here, you'll get covered with varnish and tar! As I back off I trip on some rope. What did I tell you! he says. I pick myself up and go down to the marshes where the boys used to go hunting for frogs.*

The kayak is tied to a half-submerged dock, its paddle shoved into the cockpit. I untie the line and crawl in. The kayak starts drifting downstream. Kurt appears on the bluff: he is shouting at me. The kayak moves faster. Paddle! he yells as he scrambles down the bluff. He dives into the water in his clothes but the kayak is moving more swiftly, outdistancing him. Paddle! he yells, and I push the blade into the water. It slips out of my hands and starts floating away. Suddenly there is Kurt, his face scratched and his shirt collar torn. One of his knuckles is covered with blood. He fastens the line around his shoulder and tows me back to shore. When the kayak is finally up on the sand and I'm starting to climb out he gives me a crack on the ear and the boat slams against me.

—In the morning, as Kurt was getting ready to drive back to Santa Monica, he said well, I will always feel deepest affection for you—you should probably get out of these hills, they're not good for your mind.

—Our ship steams into New York on my eighth birthday, but Father is not there to meet us. The caretaker of the mission explains that the Spirit has led him to new challenges, this time among the Navajos in the Southwest. Mother looks at him with disbelief. Franz tugs at my sleeve. I try to imagine Father preaching the gospel to a tribe of impassive Indians.

The caretaker is an elderly Pole who drags his left leg behind him, as though part of it had melted under intense heat. He says he had been a professional boxer in his youth, until alcohol almost destroyed him, but Pastor Quaile changed all that, a remarkable man, he has touched many souls—wherever he goes, Pastor Quaile touches souls. Kurt makes a strange face.

We load our luggage into three taxicabs and drive to the mission. The streets are littered with trash. The bottom floor of the mission consists of a single large dormitory. It's empty and dark. Metal cots in twin rows, as in a debtor's prison, some with mattresses, some without. Toilets and shower rooms and I AM THE WAY on the wall. Upstairs is the cafeteria, and behind it a kitchen that reeks of sour milk and rotting fruit.

Father's office is next to the kitchen. For the second time Franz tugs at my sleeve. A plain wooden desk cluttered with letters and manuscript drafts. An old typewriter. A narrow cot. A shirt hanging from a hook. The wastebasket is full of crumpled notes and brown apple cores.

—Franz has published his book. He depicts Father as a man who invented his truths and believed his inventions. Everybody gets roasted in various ways, and especially Kurt, but he saves the worst roasting for himself. He refers to himself as The Skulker. Kurt is furious and swears he will sue.

IV: 1975

—Kurt phoned in the middle of the night: I was going through Mother's belongings just now and found several sermons that Father had written as a young man. Such power in each line! We get older and things get confirmed. If you'll look at the world, Joseph, you'll see people like Franz who keep crying for food that can't nourish or heal. Be grateful for Father: he taught us to seek true sustenance.

—The evening before our scheduled departure from San Francisco Kurt drives us to Telegraph Hill. We climb out of the bus and stare down at the bay. A clear night. The buildings on Alcatraz seem to be carved out of gold. A freighter is ghosting out of the harbor and searchlights are sweeping the sky above Treasure Island. Franz points to the China Clipper.

Mother pulls up the collar of her coat. She turns to us and says: Now you see how it is. When we crossed the Atlantic I thought we would finally join him and build a new home for ourselves, but wherever we go he swims off somewhere else, like a fish keeping out of a net. For years he's been swimming like that. I don't think he is going to stop, there is some kind of need. We must find a new roof for our heads, it is time. The caravan must unpack.

Kurt says Mother, I'll stay by your side, and Franz coughs an elaborate cough.

—Franz speculates in this morning's letter about Mother's noble stoicism, which appears to him now as nothing more than a mask of a godly man's helpmeet in the best evangelical tradition:

Excerpts: *She taught us to give plausible imitations of human warmth without necessarily feeling much of anything at all. This has affected our relationships with our spouses and children, to say nothing of our friends. And because Father convinced us that the temporal world was hardly worth dealing with, being so transitory and filled with decay, we adopted a series of poses that disguised what we actually were—among them theatrical intensity and integrity-mongering à la Kurt. When Kurt looks in the mirror he starts hearing the same voices that Father used to hear, and he tries to seduce everyone with his passionate convictions, including himself.*

The self-deception of the orchestrated life. Father fled from the family in the name of the Spirit but kept photographs of us and wrote tender sentiments about Mother and the children in his journals—especially when he was thousands of miles from the domestic trap, where he could breathe easy and free. This may explain why you and I, being unable to swallow that same Spirit that Kurt keeps trying to ram down our throats, have to cling to our cold craft if we're going to function at all. Remember Jonah. Jonah had no real choice, and neither do we. When Kurt's lawyers got the court order to have my book suppressed I was ready to quit. Now I realize we must never escape from the word. What Kurt can't comprehend is that I wrote about us, all of us, with great anger and love. Every family has ruins and messages.

—When I looked at my face in the mirror this morning I saw lines everywhere. My wrist is still bad from the fall. I have a hard time holding a pencil or working the can opener.

Kurt's response to my four-page letter came this morning. Excerpts: *It was the tone of your letter, dear Joseph, that pained and distressed me. You object to the way I keep stressing the Spirit while I'm shoveling (your term) food into my mouth, and you suggest that my unhappy sexual experiences incriminate me in the eyes of the King. And then you assert that I tend to debate at such length about the importance of surrender because I have a compulsive (your term) determination to win the debate. Your implication is that the Spirit would prefer me to be more worldly and decorous—perhaps a little more like you.*

You and Franz look at people as though they are caricatures. When you try to depict me, you end up with dismissive clichés—I'm a tangle of contradictions, etc. You do this because you are frozen in your pride. I have never seen you surrender to anything—not to love, not to God, not even to the flesh. Look what Franz did to his women. Look how you've abandoned your daughter and wife. You call me a glutton: I've watched you approach a dish of meat and potatoes like a dentist.

You can't even surrender to your own manuscripts. Frozen gifts. When Franz finally published that scurrilous novel filled with slanders about me and all manner of viciousness about Father and the rest of the family, you expected me to fall to my knees in the name of aesthetics and stock that tissue of lies on my shelves. When I took legal action to preserve Father's honor you turned against me.

It must be obvious even to you, dear Joseph, that Franz has never had genuine gifts. Everything about him is calculation and artifice, and his novel would never have gone to the presses if he hadn't cleverly charmed his connections in the publishing field. Ever since he was young Franz has doubted and sneered, he has never had anything to do with our blood except criticize it, there's no warmth in the man.

Now, with even humbler gifts (if I may say so), you are trying to follow in his footsteps. Surely there are more rewarding steps to follow. I don't need any more distortions of myself and the Quaile family in my shop, and you certainly don't need any more intellectual arrogance.

My heart goes out to you both. There will never be respite for either of you until you willingly turn yourselves over to the Divine Will. But come down and visit me soon and we'll talk about this. Business has been terrible and the shop needs to be reorganized. I can't even take inventory. I keep falling into heavy depressions now that Mother is gone. We must be careful to preserve what we have.

—Spent the day in Carmel with Laura yesterday, my elbow aching constantly. We hiked through the trees at Point Lobos and peered down at the water. Several otters were cavorting about. When we got to the tip of the point we could hear the seals barking and the rattle of the surf. I asked Laura how her mother was doing. She said better. We stood at the tip of the point and watched the sun bury itself in a layer of fog. I felt something inside me had tipped to one side. Chunks of faces and years were beginning to crumble down into the sea.

As we were driving home Laura looked at my face. She said you must be tired, you should see the bags under your eyes.

—Franz writes that he is trying to teach himself all the things he's been urging on me. We must learn to discard. The great thing is to give things away.

Another bad night. I wake up to the feeling that somebody is in the room. I turn on the lights. The room is empty. I kick off the blankets and light a cigarette. 3:07 A.M. A sudden pang over Laura and Claire. I go into the living room and turn on the TV. Fred Astaire and Ginger Rogers are doing the Castle Walk. The tube drains the blood out of me.

—Every night I hear Franz in his cramped tower room: long pauses of silence, then the clack-clack of the typewriter keys, then the silence again. Kurt says that typewriter's driving me out of my mind, he's deliberately torturing me! Mother says come eat some soup.

Father appears only twice, both times unannounced and in haste. The moment he steps through the door I can feel the uneasiness rippling from him through the house. Mother becomes quiet and sombre in his presence. His face is criss-crossed with deep lines and his teeth show decay.

His questions are forced, clearly contrived, and his voice remains strained except when he loses himself in his descriptions of the most recent spiritual feasts. He says the old Polish boxer has finally passed on to his reward, God be praised, but the mission keeps getting vandalized by hooligans and the forces of Darkness and it's going to be razed.

He asks how the various children are doing, especially Kurt, who is surely preparing himself for the Glorious Call, but soon after Mother starts filling him in I can see his eyes clouding and his mind begins twisting through underground tunnels that no one can follow or reach. Both times he departs with his battered suitcase I feel troubled by what I have seen. My dreams seem to circle around me: dead animals, water, hunger and lust.

—Hiked around Angel Island with Laura today, the full loop this time. When we came upon the defunct army base on the east side I went off by myself and poked around the yellow PX and the mission-style guardhouse, the chapel, the gutted officers' quarters, the empty shell of the three-story hospital—walls blistered, the urinals coldly exposed, a sense of strength slowly relinquished, those thousands of voices and boots, the fences gouged open and rusting, the glass smashed—while off in the distance, as though nothing has happened, the jets whine through the mist and the Richmond refineries smoke. I couldn't get my head straight for the rest of the day. All those windows that once had held glass. I took Laura home and drove back to my apartment. I awoke in the middle of the night, the room turning with dreams.

—Franz phoned last night sounding very distraught. He had just learned through Max that Kurt had been arrested last week for soliciting sexual favors of a couple of L.A. police decoys following a spiritual feast in Ventura where people were speaking in tongues. Kurt insists he is going to fight this—he claims his intentions were deliberately misconstrued. I asked Franz if Kurt was in jail. He said no, they released him on bail—I'm catching a flight to L.A. Saturday, come and meet me down there.

—I didn't recognize Franz when I knocked on his door at the airport motel. His face sagged in sections, as though it were gradually stretching apart, and he leaned to one side as he walked. His hair was disheveled. He said we can talk later, let's go.

We got to Santa Monica in the late afternoon. Kurt's house was boarded up, a NO TRESPASSING HAZARDOUS AREA notice on the front door. Almost the entire back yard had slid off and the house's foundations were exposed. The Pacific was hammering below. We drove to the bookstore.

The shop was closed and the lights were off, but I could see Kurt inside, heating something on an electric hot plate. A sleeping bag lay rolled up in a corner. Franz rapped on the window. Kurt shouted I'm closed! without turning around. Franz kept rapping. Finally Kurt unplugged the hot plate and shuffled forward. He peered through the glass. He hadn't shaved for several days. He cocked his head slightly and blinked.

As he opened the door he didn't seem surprised. He said Joseph, the shop is a mess, you'll be able to give me a hand. Franz stepped forward. Kurt looked at his face. He switched on the lights and said well, come on in.

Kleinvogel in San Francisco

I'd completely forgotten about all the different hats my friend Albert Kleinvogel used to wear when things were still positive between us, before he got so withdrawn and intense and eventually broke down at the party we threw him in Tiburon a few weeks ago. For the first three or four years we were sharing the cottage on Telegraph Hill Kleinvogel was always wearing *something* on his head—I think the hats made him feel taller—but then he started withdrawing, he let his racquetball membership lapse and quit sailing with me, and he also stopped paying attention to his clothes and I totally forgot about all that headgear of his until yesterday, when I found his post card in my mailbox:

Dear Stan—

Resting up at my sister's on Long Island Sound. I've gone through some of my father's old letters to her: no further clues. I doubt I'll be returning to San Francisco so please clean out my closets & sell everything for my share of the rent (help yourself to whatever you can't unload). Sorry about Tiburon, it was building up for a long time. Mitzi found this card in one of my father's circus scrapbooks from the European tours. Al.

The post card was a 1926 portrait of Benito Mussolini in a frock coat and a stiff shirt with one of those turned-up collars that bend down at the tips, I can never remember their name, and I thought to myself: holy cats, Mussolini again, I give up on that guy! About a year and a half ago Kleinvogel developed a kind of obsession about the Italian Fascists while doing research on his father and The Flying Kleinvogels and I honestly think it affected his mind. I tossed the card into the wastebasket and started checking his closets. He probably thought he was doing me some kind of big favor by inviting me to help myself to whatever I wouldn't be able to unload. That was so characteristic of him. It was obvious he didn't have anything worth keeping except maybe his ancient Remington portable, which wasn't much good any more, and his clothes wouldn't fit me, of course. One thing about Al Kleinvogel, he's the type of extreme narcissist who is constantly turning his back on objective reality and getting tripped up instead on his private mind games. Mussolini, for example. All the time I had known him, which was over ten years, he was terribly self-centered and out of touch with the here-and-now, which is typical, of course, of a lot of short men, but as I kept rummaging through his things yesterday I kept getting the feeling I was perceiving him for the first time, I mean his true inner self. There had always been a peculiar tension in him I had never been able to pin down or explain, and I started to brood over it. I don't like to brood as a rule because brooding tends to scramble your energy field and it weakens your grip on what's happening *now,* which is all anyone's got when you think about it, but there were destructive impulses inside Al Kleinvogel I felt I had to confront for myself because I didn't want to end up like that.

I dragged the large carton marked HATS from his closet, and when I pried the lid open, sure enough, there were the hats, and suddenly I was getting these intuitive flashes that there was something *significant* about all that stuff in the carton but I wasn't sure what, so I took the box into the living room and grabbed my notebook and wrote out an itemized list:

1 Greek sailor's cap, black
1 SF Giants cap
1 deerstalker hat
2 celluloid sun visors, orange & maroon
1 Borsalino, cream-colored

1 Intl Harvester tractor-driver's cap
1 floppy leather hat w/silver hatband
3 tennis visors, white
1 top hat, to go w/opera tails
1 leather sun visor, hand-tooled
1 Mao cap, blue
2 sweatbands, red/white/blue
1 Rex Harrison tweed hat
1 sailor's watch cap, black
1 Daffy Duck cap w/torn bill
1 Panama hat, white
1 US Army fatigue cap w/anti-war buttons
1 sombrero, dark purple w/gold trim
1 cyclist's cap w/Peugeot emblem

At the bottom of the carton was his scuba mask minus the snorkel, a pair of Speedo swimming goggles, some blue-tinted sunglasses with a missing lens and the frayed Adidas he'd wear when we'd go sailing on San Francisco Bay in my Coronado 25. I tried on some of the hats but of course they were too small. When my girlfriend Colleen came over for dinner that night she examined the hats and went digging around through his other closets and brought out the elegant tails he used to wear to the Opera House, along with the matching black Dracula cape the Filipino tailor had made to order, and she said Stan, it's no wonder he finally got himself so unglued, the majority of undersized men have really serious problems about self-acceptance, it just goes with their height.

Kleinvogel happens to be just a shade under five foot one in his socks, which is probably the fundamental reality he has never been able to accept about himself, it's affected every serious relationship he's ever attempted, especially with women, and eventually it eroded whatever connection there had been between us.

I met him in the fall of 1967, the day I started working at

Hesperides Press. His desk was right next to mine. Hesperides is a small publishing house in the heart of San Francisco's Financial District, just around the corner from Tadich Grill, and for years it had been cranking out little pamphlets and books offering gardening tips and cooking hints and suggestions on West Coast motoring excursions, stuff like that, but some fresh blood came in just before I arrived on the scene, two extremely sharp guys from L.A. who were hot on expanding the market by pushing into terrain that was intellectually more challenging and relevant to the times, like exploring what, exactly, a person might need for a really dynamic lifestyle—what kind of products might enhance self-realization and what some of the inner disciplines might be—which is why I got hired. I didn't know anything about putting in patios or building barbecue pits, but I'd majored in Cultural Restructuring at Petaluma State and had managed to publish a series of articles on holistic athletics in a local bi-weekly which made some impact around the Bay Area, and Hesperides grabbed me on the spot. Kleinvogel had been with them for a couple of years, editing travel guides and writing booklets aimed at the higher-priced backpacking market, and the new guys from L.A. figured they would put us together and come up with a natural team. Kleinvogel would enlighten the readers on what kinds of mountaineering tents to purchase for the Sierras and which hiking boots to invest in, while I'd handle the wilderness self-exploration adventures and the high-altitude innerspace needs.

We hit it off pretty well, Al and I, because he was almost as much into physical fitness as I was, and we managed to generate a nice easy flow whenever we worked out together, which was just about every day at that time. For such an unusually short person Kleinvogel was really a fine athlete, he had great coordination and fine muscle tone for a guy in his mid-thirties. When I remarked on that once he said well,

Stan, I was practically born and raised in the circus, you know—I was doing high-wire work with my parents and Mitzi my sister from the time I was seven or eight, so taking care of my body just comes natural to me.

At least it was for a while. Almost right from the first day I met him I kept noticing these strange little tensions in him. Maybe having to travel around with the circus as a kid damaged him, and maybe his father was partly to blame. I remember one day Al was telling me about his memories of the circus, and he scratched his head at one point and said you know, Stan, my father was very tight-lipped—in some ways he was really a very strange man. So maybe some of that rubbed off on Al, I don't know. It was like there was always a little barb festering in his side and he couldn't yank it out.

His few tangible gripes seemed pretty illogical to me. He told me, for example, that he wasn't too crazy about his job, he called it crass huckstering, and he said that the mountains and streams were just a part of the hype, but in spite of that negative attitude he would work like a son of a bitch—much too hard, as a matter of fact, which is one of the first flaws I spotted in him: his compulsiveness on the job. When he was editing a manuscript or pounding away on the typewriter he was virtually impossible to reach, you just couldn't get through to the guy. I kept trying to get him to lighten up a bit, and for a while I was actually getting somewhere—that was when we moved into the cottage together—but now that I think back on it I can see that the negative spaces were always just under the surface in him.

That whole Telegraph Hill episode with Kleinvogel was a very frustrating experience for me. A few weeks after I joined the Hesperides team I got a lead on this rustic little cottage on the east slope of Telegraph Hill, and when I showed it to Kleinvogel and suggested we go half and half on the rent he said yes. He'd been living in the Mission District, in a grim little room above a Mexican restaurant on Valencia

Street, and he took just one look at the cottage and saw his big chance to get away from the tortillas, and before I knew what was happening he had grabbed the glassed-in sun porch for himself without even discussing it with me, leaving me with the bedroom in back, which was smaller and had just one window facing into the hill. Kleinvogel's sun porch was surrounded by fuschias and had a marvelous view of the bay and the hills of Marin to the north, and of course I couldn't afford to rent the place just on my salary so I kept my mouth shut about his grabbing the sun porch, but that kind of revealed to me how self-centered he could be.

It didn't take us long to fix up the place. I was starting to make some meaningful connections with a few of the women at work, so I bought a good waterbed and installed my sound system, and we fixed up the living room with house plants and pillows and candles and a color TV, and pretty soon we were settled and having some really fine times. Whenever we felt like splurging or impressing some new lady we would pig out up at Julius' Castle, which was literally a stone's throw away—on windless nights you could actually hear the dishes clattering in their kitchen—and after dinner we'd kind of float back to the cottage and smoke some Colombian gold and then float down the stairs to the bottom of the hill and catch the Dixieland band over at Pier 23. I also managed to finagle a low-interest loan and bought the Coronado 25, which came complete with a berth at the tip of Richardson Bay in Sausalito, and we got ourselves a couple of Peugeot ten-speed bikes and joined the racquetball club next to The Cannery, and Kleinvogel started collecting all these various hats and fancy sun visors and the good times were starting to roll.

But like I said, there was always this tension in him, he could never completely relax, not even when we were tacking around Angel Island or coasting down Mount Tamalpais on our bikes, and it occurred to me then that his main problem was simple, he just couldn't get over being so short, he was constantly checking himself in windows and mirrors, always measuring and comparing, especially when some good-looking woman was around. And it wasn't as though he couldn't line up an occasional score when he set his mind to it, because lots of nights we would go to some party or maybe some disco emporium and I'd watch him rev up his razzle-dazzle machinery, and for a while he was actually getting into a whole string of encounters with some stunning females. But there was still this damaged part of him way deep inside and it just wouldn't heal. I happen to be five foot four and three-quarters, which isn't exactly the top of the line, but it is an acceptable size if you stay in good shape, and of course staying fit has always been like a sacred commitment to me, since the body is the temple of the soul—but five one, that's a definite problem, and Kleinvogel just didn't seem to have the inner resources to deal with that problem. The point is that my height has never been any *issue* with me, any more than the color of my eyes or the shape of my nose, and it certainly hasn't made me compulsive or strained. If anyone was ever driven, Al Kleinvogel was driven, especially after he started working on that book about The Flying Kleinvogels and began asking questions about the Italian Fascists, and his final weird reaction in Tiburon really opened my eyes. I will never allow that to happen to me, I mean life is too short, it just isn't worth it.

I don't know about those hats of his: maybe they were some kind of neurotic cosmetic for him, or like quick costume changes, which made me think later that he had never really developed a viable identity for himself. The funny thing of it is that very few of the hats really worked well for him. He liked to wear the Greek sailor's cap when we were out on the bay, for example, which wasn't too practical because the wind was always blowing it off his head, but I think he kept wearing it because he figured it had the right rakish look for the Whaler's Dock over in Tiburon, where we'd usually tie up on Sundays and drink gin and scrutinize the tanned ladies until dinnertime. Kleinvogel would wear the cap low, so you couldn't see his eyes, and it was common for him not to utter a word for an hour, sometimes more than an hour, he'd just sit there and study the women from behind his sunglasses and drink. When the sun started setting we'd float inside and dig into some scampi or calamari, along with a bottle or two of chablis, and by the time we were sailing back to Sausalito it'd be dark out on Richardson Bay and we'd be stumbling all over the lines and laughing and having a ball. Of course we'd end up with some banging and scraping as we brought the boat in, but it wasn't too serious, and even the scraping was somehow memorable.

Just about every hat had a story behind it, and some of the stories were pretty negative. He had picked up the floppy leather concoction with the silver band at a rock concert in Santa Cruz, but it didn't last very long. For a while Al and I were catching a lot of rock concerts and bluegrass festivals all over the Bay Area, but one day we were down in Monterey listening to some really high-powered groups and he started to grumble and complained that his left ear was bothering him, he said he was getting too old for that amplified overkill, it was affecting his ears, and when we got home he threw the leather hat into the carton and never wore it again.

He got the Rex Harrison number for the winter months, when we'd go racing up to West Marin in my battered old Porsche and poke around Point Reyes and Bolinas and places like that in the rain, but that hat never really looked good on him—I told him he was coming across as a nervous Jewish boy trying to appear very British—and he glanced in the mirror and said Stanley, you're right, I don't know what's the matter with me, and he put the Rex Harrison away. The Giants cap came a bit later, and it revealed something else that was strange about him. Whenever Kleinvogel and I would decide to check out some new pub where the action was good he would get himself into some pretty wild clothes. He said he liked to create incongruent effects—that was his term, *incongruent effects*—and that accounts for the orange and black Giants cap and the celluloid visors and the big Borsalino and all the rest of it. But he didn't seem really suited for hats in the first place, they simply called more attention to his size, and sometimes they would even backfire on him. Like one night he was wearing the deerstalker to the Electric Generator on Union Street and some enormous black dude in a luminous tank top lumbered up to him while he was dancing with a long-legged Eurasian. The black dude picked him up like a cat and said Sherlock, I've been hunting all over for you, where the hell have you been, let's go home for a Watson massage! Kleinvogel brought the guy down to his knees with a beautiful karate chop right in the groin, but he never wore the deerstalker after that.

He was also experimenting with scarves and cravats and tried smoking a pipe for a while, but his face was too small for a pipe. He got into the habit of wearing three-piece suits to the office, he said Stanley, a suit with a vest has got natural clout, but he'd top off the suit with some kind of weird thing like the purple sombrero or the tractor-driver cap.

Then one August he decided he had to have a set of tails for the upcoming opera season, he had never had tails and he really felt ready for a nice set of tails. Of course he had a hard time locating tails small enough to fit him, but he finally tracked down a pair in a spooky little shop in an alley smack in the heart of the old Barbary Coast. The Filipino tailor specialized in funeral attire for children and very small adults, so Kleinvogel finally had his tails and the lined Dracula cape. People snickered at him in the Opera House, and he never felt really comfortable in his tails, and eventually he put them away.

It was around the same time that he bought his tails from the Filipino that I started running around with Colleen. I had met her on the Golden Gate Marathon Race and we discovered we had really incredible rapport, and I was also attracted to her because I'd never been involved with a tall skinny redhead before, so I started to spend more and more time with her. This left Kleinvogel with a lot of free time on his hands, which must have made him feel nervous, I mean he could never just relax and lay back, he always had to be doing *something* every minute of the day, and so he started researching the book he'd been meaning to write about The Flying Kleinvogels and their life with the circus on two continents. He sent out dozens of letters to his relatives both here and abroad, and to various circus people who had worked with his parents, and we saw less and less of each other after that, especially since Colleen turned out to be a very active individual, she had all kinds of social and political commitments, whereas Kleinvogel was just a natural loner at heart. Colleen and I managed to talk him into driving down to Pacific Grove with us for a conference on the otter problem, and we tried to get him involved in the Western Addition Food Conspiracy and the automotive repair co-op out in the Avenues, things like that, and he actually attended a few meetings, kind of grudgingly, of course, but his heart wasn't in it at all. I always suspected he was feeling some kind of ambivalent attraction for Colleen because she was so assertive and such a knockout to look at in her frazzled and hypertense way, but they were constantly getting into ridiculous arguments about urban terrorism and nuclear energy and the new consciousness, things like that, with him always playing the role of the skeptic, of course, and one day the three of us drove across the bay to a Maoist Solidarity poetry reading in downtown Oakland, and he bought himself a little blue Mao cap and stayed half an hour and then whispered hey, Stanley, I'm going to Jack London Square, and slipped out. As soon as the reading was over we started hunting for him, and we finally found him in a little bar on the fringes of Jack London Square with his Mao cap on backwards and a bottle of Coors in his hand. Colleen said well, what the hell are you doing in here? He said drinking, Colleen, I'm just drinking some beer. So she got really disgusted with him and informed him that he was an escapist from life and a political parasite, stuff like that, and his wearing the cap backwards wasn't funny at all, and I kept them apart after that.

Of course we were still doing a few things together, he and I, like scuba diving occasionally down at Point Lobos and keeping up with our lunch-hour racquetball routine, and every once in a while we'd still walk up to Julius' Castle and just pig out and talk, but there was definite distancing going on between us and he seemed to be getting much harder to reach. More and more he'd just lapse into silence and stare out at nothing in particular, as though listening for something somewhere. I'd ask him what's wrong and he'd blink and say nothing's wrong, Stan. It was really unnerving. Sometimes he'd get into depressions that would go on for three or four days and I'd see the dark look right away in his eyes, even down in the office, he'd just sit at his desk with some manuscript in front of him and listen and stare.

One good thing about Hesperides, it's always been an employee-oriented operation, we've had profit-sharing for years and the energy level is incredibly high. Everyone is constantly organizing birthday parties and moonlight cruises around Alcatraz and picnics on Angel Island, things like that, and of course we all go, it helps keep us in touch with each other and brings a human dimension to the team. When I first met Kleinvogel he'd put on quite a show at the parties and come across really funny and make people laugh, but especially after that Maoist poetry reading in Oakland I noticed him getting more moody and strained, and he didn't socialize quite as much as before. He also got into the strange habit of stiffening his legs whenever there were people around, as though trying to force one more inch out of them, and although he kept flashing his bright boyish grins I got the feeling the smiles were mechanical and he was flashing them out of sheer habit. He also started getting nervous in restaurants, or at least very uneasy, which never happened before, and I noticed it'd take him a long time to settle down, I mean he'd keep shifting his weight, twisting this way and that until he'd managed to tuck one leg under himself, which gave him a couple more inches, I suppose, and made him feel more secure.

He also got to be compulsive about food. He developed this concern about not wasting a scrap and would literally devour everything on his plate, even if it was lousy or burnt to a crisp, and at home I'd sometimes catch him actually *licking* his plate when he didn't think I was looking. And his compulsiveness took other peculiar forms. Magazines, for example—he had subscriptions to half a dozen periodicals like *Harper's* and *The Atlantic* and *The New York Review of Books* and would force himself to plow through them from cover to cover without missing a line. Sometimes he would take a whole weekend to catch up on back issues, and he'd mumble and pull at his hair as he checked off each page with his red ballpoint pen. What I'm trying to say is that the poor little guy had a natural tendency to go overboard on just about everything, he was like a bad faucet that gives you zero or comes on full blast.

One odd thing about him, he never paid much attention to his shoes. Most short men are very conscious about their shoes, but Kleinvogel refused to wear platforms or boots, he used to call them clodhoppers for turkeys, but the problem of his height kept on bothering him, and it came out in various ways. One night we had floated home half-juiced from the Cliff House and I switched on the TV and there was Jimmy Cagney in some early movie shoving a grapefruit into his leading lady's face, and Kleinvogel sat down on the couch with his head in his hands and said no, no I couldn't do that, Stan, that isn't my style, it just wouldn't be me! Which wasn't entirely true, because I had a few opportunities here and there to observe him with women, including Colleen, and I noticed right away that the more he would care for some woman the bitchier he'd get. He was definitely most mellow with people he really disliked, or at least he put on the best act with them. Whenever he was around anyone he just couldn't stand he'd be super-deferential and self-deprecating and throw out wide-eyed leading questions and pretend to lap up the responses, and behind his politeness you could practically *smell* his impatience and silent contempt.

I think his remarkable scoring with women was tied in to this neurotic compulsion he had to pretend to be interested and concerned. I've noticed that women seem to relate best to men who can act sympathetic without seeming threatening, and that was Al's formula all the way. I used to watch him in action, especially when we were into this biofeedback phase for a while with a group up on Nob Hill, and I was struck by how fast he could get some of those Anglican women to start paying attention to him. I guess they liked working on his body because he was so small and innocent-looking and easy to roll over and rearrange, and of course he would always go along with whatever kind of biofeedback exercises they felt like exploring, and before the women knew it they would find themselves getting all maternal and steamy over him, it was real Freudian, and he couldn't fight them off with a club after that. He told me one Sunday morning after spending a hair-raising night with the wife of a dentist from Cupertino that he was deliberately getting back at tall men by getting it on with their girlfriends and wives, it was one way of tilting the balance his way. I said holy cats, Al, you have got to be kidding! He said no, I'm not kidding at all, Stan, I'm working my way up the ladder, you watch.

I could never really understand this hostility he developed

for tall men, I mean his reasoning was so convoluted. He had apparently come to the conclusion that most tall men were boors, they were very low-level in body and mind and were natural popinjays, and he said he had empirical proof. When our phone would start ringing very early in the morning, or maybe in the middle of the night, Kleinvogel would shuffle out of his sun porch screaming *I've got it! I've got it!* and of course it'd be a wrong number and he'd swear up and down that the caller had been at least six foot two, maybe more, he could tell by his supercilious tone. He often told me that people out here on the West Coast, especially tall people, had a terrible habit of ringing you up at all hours of the day and night and then babbling on and on without even considering if you're tied up or not, it's like time has no meaning for them. Sometimes he'd get into a regular diatribe on tall men. One day we were hiking the Steep Ravine trail down Mount Tam to Stinson Beach and he said Stan, have you ever figured out why pomposity comes so naturally to tall men— I mean have you noticed how a typical six-footer will just *automatically* sink his ass into your best chair with a self-satisfied grunt, and have you noticed how they're constantly sucking their thumbs? If you study child psychology, Stan, you'll discover that their mothers encourage them to suck on their thumbs from the time they are born, it's like they get the idea they're blessing humanity with royal infants or something, just because they're so huge. They certainly act like a privileged class, I mean they ram their beefy elbows into you when you sit next to them in a theater, and they tromple on your feet and make all kinds of noises and fart something awful, and on top of that they're messy as hell. Have you noticed that, Stan? They're like big messy brats, they are constantly leaving their messes behind! I mean take a good look at my desk at Hesperides. You know I don't smoke, Stan, so who do you suppose leaves those cigarette ashes all over my desk, or the butts in the paper clip tray, or those styrofoam cups with cold coffee? And another thing: bathrooms! Next time we go to a party at somebody's house you keep your eye on the bathroom. Every tall man I've ever encountered leaves the toilet seat up! That's a fact, Stan, their mothers *train* them that way, it's like they've got to establish their natural superiority! So naturally these great big thumbsuckers never bother to bus their dirty dishes in cafeterias because they feel that's beneath them, and they're insolent with waiters and newspaper vendors, and I'll tell you something else, Stan, it's like there's some kind of law of genetics that says boy, you are going to pay for your height—and they pay! You want to know *how* they pay? If you do some research on the subject you will quickly discover that tall people have never been very creative, I mean not in a top-drawer sense, that's a well-documented historical fact! They make passable flunky executives and managers, they're so goddamned officious and smug, but the fact is they're not very sharp and they've never been very creative—when we get home I'll show you the proof!

His so-called proof was a new low for him, it was so totally off-the-wall. For weeks he'd been secluding himself in his sun porch at night, compiling a catalogue of Eminent Short Men on little cards which he kept in a long metal box. I said what about women, Al, where are the girls? He said well, Stan, most women are naturally short and I don't want to get into questions of sexism or stacking the deck, so I'm leaving them out. There was absolutely no logic to his list, it wasn't chronological or alphabetical or anything else—the only apparent criteria he used were that all of the men had been (a) famous, and (b) short. I tried to point out a few of the fallacies in his selections. Toscanini and Gandhi were passable candidates, but I argued that Alexander Pope didn't really qualify, and neither did Toulouse-Lautrec, because they were both cripples and cripples are hardly a fair category, they are physical freaks, but Kleinvogel said no, short is short and the cripples are part of the picture, and then, just to nail down his point, he added Charles Steinmetz to his list.

He carried that list to outrageous extremes. One very hot day we were sharing a pitcher of beer at the Mountain Home Inn on Mount Tam and Kleinvogel got into a lengthy discussion with a red-faced little Jesuit priest who'd just hiked up from Mill Valley. One thing led to another and we drank some more beer and then the priest said well, yes, he could really go along with the idea that creativity is concentrated in very short men. Then he lowered his voice and said fellows, did you know that recent investigations in the Vatican have disclosed that the historical Christ was *maximum* five foot six, and he had a large aquiline nose and weak eyes, but they're keeping the facts under wraps because millions of simple believers would have a terrible time overhauling their lifelong preconceptions. I couldn't believe what I was hearing, and after the priest slipped into his knapsack and took off for the summit I said Al, do you really believe that the historical Christ bore a striking resemblance to Woody Allen? Al squinted at the pitcher of beer for a minute and then quietly reached for a paper napkin and added Woody Allen's name to his list. I said Al, I would hardly describe Woody Allen as an Eminent Short Man. He said well, Stan, I think you're just wrong—Woody Allen is certainly qualified, he's a lot better qualified than most, and I'll tell you something else, I'll bet he never leaves the toilet seat up!

There was something ironic and obviously self-destructive about his compiling that list. I mean you'd expect him to mellow and feel more secure as he tried to convince himself that shorter is better, but instead he put in longer hours than ever before at Hesperides Press and seemed even more driven and unhappy with himself, and it was right around this time, when he was hunting up names for his list, that he totally stopped paying attention to his clothes. I remember one afternoon in particular, it was a foggy Saturday and I had talked him into doing some long-distance swimming with me at Aquatic Park, and so we swam a couple of miles in the fog while the bongo drummers up on the sunbathing terraces kept pounding away on their drums, and then we got out of the water and were drying ourselves when he suddenly kind of froze and blinked up at the very top terrace, above all the drummers and junkies and freaks. He was staring at a small wrinkled man with a wispy mustache who was leaning against the back wall. The little guy looked like a dandy, he was wearing white slacks and a blazer with some kind of heraldic device on the pocket and had a light blue bandana or scarf around his neck, and I could see he was giving one of the bongo drummers the eye. Kleinvogel turned away and went back to drying himself, but that night he got very depressed and collected all the rest of his visors and hats and threw them into the box.

I tried to snap him out of it by getting him to sign up for a night course out at San Francisco State, but that also backfired on him. What happened was that Colleen and I had signed up for this Creative Writing course that met two nights a week and I talked Al into taking a crack at it, I said it'd help motivate him to really get moving on his book on The Flying Kleinvogels, and so the button got pushed and he started to write. The workshop was being directed by a genuine survivor of the Beat Generation, a mad poet named Wolf Gelbendorf who was constantly full of weird visions and strange prophecies. Kleinvogel turned sour as usual, and after two or three sessions he said Stan, I can't stand to hear that hairy clown read his mystical gibberish any more, all those cosmic epiphanies are just hot air and smoke and I'm sick of that whole workshop scene—I just can't write for a group, the whole process has got to be private for me, all that poking and sharing just freezes me up! I said Al, you're a real misanthrope. He said maybe I am, but I don't need Wolf Gelbendorf yowling his poems at me. So he dropped out of the workshop but kept moving ahead on The Flying Kleinvogels on his own, which is probably one of the reasons he finally broke down—he absolutely refused any kind of external support and put a big overload on his brain.

The first part of the book was actually fairly easy for him, he was simply transcribing the facts he'd researched, and I have to admit it was pretty dry stuff. His father and mother were both Viennese Jews with a long circus heritage. They'd organized their own act, The Flying Kleinvogels, back in the early Twenties, long before Al had been born, and toured around Europe with various circuses for about fifteen years—until they sensed another war building up and made the move to the States. So Al and Mitzi got almost all of their early schooling on the road, mostly from their mother, and by the time they were in their mid-teens they were getting equal billing, which may account at least partly for his crippling narcissism. Then in the Fifties his father decided they'd switch from their standard trapeze work to high-wire bicycle acts, which were tricky but actually less strenuous, and because he wanted a risk-factor to draw in the crowds he insisted on working without any net, but that turned out to be an unfortunate move. During the summer of 1957 they were working the eastern seaboard from New England to Florida, and one gusty afternoon in Atlantic City the old man broke his neck when the wind hit his bike and he fell sixty feet. He was conscious just long enough to mumble something about a safety deposit box in a bank in Manhattan, and then he was gone. The mother retired to a mobile-home park in Orlando and died in a head-on collision the following July. Mitzi married a civil engineer from Long Island and proceeded to raise a fine son and a house full of cats. Al bounced around from one job to another and managed to pick up an English degree from NYU and made his way to the

West Coast—he had heard that San Francisco had a nice lively tempo and was open to genuine talent regardless of background or business connections, which sounded promising to him.

His one big regret, he confessed to me one night after he had been drinking some wine, was allowing himself to get stuck at Hesperides Press. He said the job doesn't have any purpose or edge, Stan—I just can't imagine myself spending year after year writing car-camping tips and descriptions of Western ghost towns. I said Al, you're your worst enemy, you look at everything in such a negative light. He just shrugged.

His real breakdown didn't come until later, of course, and the catalyst, oddly enough, was Colleen. One night she dropped over to drink rum and watch Creature Features with me. Al was furiously pounding away on his typewriter out on the sun porch, and as I was getting the rum she slipped in there—mainly to bug him, I suppose—and started reading aloud this portion of the manuscript he'd just finished typing, about how his parents would sign up with some outfit doing the Scandinavian circuit every summer, and then as they'd get into autumn they would work their way south, commencing the Italian run around the first week of October and finishing the whole Mediterranean sweep by the following February or March. Colleen must have noticed she was getting on Kleinvogel's nerves because she kept right on reading, and when she got to a section where he had listed his father's fraternal organizations and clubs she stopped and looked puzzled and re-read one of the lines: *Heroism and Holiness Guild, Rome: 1925–1940*. I was watching them from the next room and I could see she was turning her wheels, she seemed to be trying to remember something. She said Al, what's this Holiness Guild? He said look, I'm really busy right now, I don't know anything about the Holiness Guild, he never talked about it—we found the membership cards in his safety deposit box after he died. She said boy, this rings some kind of bell in the back of my mind, I was studying this ten years ago, I'll just have to dig out my old notes.

The next night she came back looking pleased with herself and announced that the Heroism and Holiness Guild had been founded on April 12, 1925, as an auxiliary of the Fascist Party by none other than the top man himself. When Al heard that he just stared at her. She said Al, this is going to help sell your book, it's a dynamite angle—a Jewish circus performer gets swept up by the Fascist mystique! Al said stop, just hold on for a minute, you've got documentation on this? She said hey, it's a matter of record. He said bring me the documentation, Colleen. She said sure.

Her documentation, it turned out, was very sketchy, just a couple of lines that didn't explain anything about the Guild. Al had to know more. I tried to point out that he was working himself into a state, he was getting upset over something that happened a long time ago, but he pushed me aside and went into the sun porch with his reference books. I said to Colleen Christ, he's falling apart. She said well, he's pretty unstable, you know.

I decided to leave him alone for a while, but he got worse and worse. One windy afternoon I tried to get him to go jogging down to the Ferry Building with me, he was looking so haggard and drawn, but he just gave me a blank look and started rambling about how his father must have had *some* kind of reason for getting mixed up with that Guild and maintaining his membership clear up to 1940, when it must have been pretty obvious what was happening to the Jews. I said holy cats, Al, I just can't comprehend why you're doing all this to yourself, get your running shoes on! He said Stan, I am going to find out why he joined, what it meant, why he kept the connection so long, why he kept the whole business a secret right up to the day he got knocked off the bike, and why he hung on to those membership cards, all goddamn sixteen of them, instead of tearing them up—I mean those membership cards must have *meant* something to him: were they some kind of signal to us, or to somebody else? But what was the message, Stan? What was he trying to say?

I laced up my sneakers and went out for my run, and when I came back Al was back in his sun porch again. I turned on the TV and fixed dinner for myself and broke open a bottle of good Mountain Red, and when I had smoked my last joint around midnight and switched off the TV he was still at his desk taking notes, totally over the rainbow again.

Some of the people at work started getting alarmed over his personality change, they wondered if there was something psychosomatic going on, or if something was happening upstairs. It was virtually impossible to get him to go out to our usual hangouts any more, but I did make one big final effort to try to lighten him up and get him back to the real world again. His birthday was just around the corner and I thought it'd be therapeutic if I could get him to do some sailing with me, like in the old days. Then I got the idea that a bunch of us from Hesperides could spring a surprise birthday party on him, and the Whaler's Dock in Tiburon was the logical place, he just wouldn't expect it and it'd be like a quick burst of positive energy and maybe open his eyes to what he was doing to himself.

I talked to a few people and we set it up for the following Saturday, and then Colleen got into the picture and said let's go all the way with a seafood buffet, we can make this an absolute blast. So we made the arrangements and everything was in place, but when Saturday rolled around I had a hell of a time convincing him to go sailing with me, he said he had just run across new material on the Jewish situation under the Fascists but the articles were written in French and Italian and it was taking him forever to decipher the texts. I told him I just had to tune up the rigging on the boat, it was way overdue, and of course I couldn't do it myself. Well, he tugged at his hair and said let's do it fast, Stan, I'm really caught up in this thing.

We sailed out of Richardson Bay to the mouth of the Gate and when I started to tack towards Alameda he said hey, what is this? I said Al, I can't tune all the rigging at once, take it easy, okay?—have a beer. He helped himself to a beer and stretched out on the deck and before we had passed Treasure Island he had fallen asleep with the can of beer still in his hand. I took the boat under the Bay Bridge and up the Oakland Estuary, just to kill a little time, and then came about and headed for Tiburon.

The sun was starting to set when we finally tied up but the air was still warm. Everybody was there, of course, out on the platform, yelling happy birthday and generally whooping it up, and Al gasped and awoke and just stared for a while, and then he got to his feet and we jumped off the boat and, sure enough, he started smiling and nodding and letting himself get kissed and I felt really good, I could see he was honestly trying to come out of his shell.

Then the party shifted into high gear and more people arrived and I lost track of him for a while. Everybody was having a marvelous time. It got dark pretty soon and the night breezes started to come in in sudden little puffs, they were riffling the napkins on the tables and knocking the plastic glasses over on their sides, so the crowd went inside and started attacking the seafood buffet. Colleen looked around and said hey, where's the cute little acrobat boy? I told her to get off his case and started hunting around for him.

I finally found him outside, perched up on a pile at the end of the dock like a gull. A yawl was just cutting through the yacht harbor with its running lights on and San Francisco was glittering across the bay, and it was getting really chilly outside so I said holy cats, it's *your* party, you know—come inside and get something to eat, they're all waiting for you. When he looked down at me I could see that his face was incredibly strained. He said untie the boat, Stan, we've stayed long enough, you promised we wouldn't be gone very long and I've got to get back to my work. I said oh, Jesus Christ, they all went to a lot of trouble and expense to put this together for you and you can't even make an appearance, what's the matter with you—I'm not going to haul up the sails and take off when the party's just getting warmed up, there's a birthday cake waiting for you!

He didn't say anything, he just sat there on top of that pile and stared out at the bay. I nudged him a little and said Al, it's your birthday, come on! He said Stanley, it isn't my party, are you going to untie the boat? I said man, I give up—I have tried, I have tried, I've been trying for years and I'm just sick of trying any more, you can't tell me that I haven't tried! I felt like knocking him off that damn pile. I said Al, you have never been able to accept what you are and it's killing you now, take a look at your face, I'm disgusted with you, I mean what are you trying to *prove?*

I started to go back inside and then there was this splash and I turned around and saw he was swimming towards San Francisco—he hadn't even bothered to take off his sneakers. I yelled at him but he kept right on swimming, using his usual sharp little kicks. Then I remember there was lots of confusion and somebody was calling for the cops, and then the bartender came running out and jumped into a dinghy and I jumped in behind him and untied the line. The bartender fitted the oars into the oarlocks and started to row.

The wind had really picked up and the whitecaps were striking the side of the dinghy, getting both of us wet, and I kept yelling to Kleinvogel but he was out of the harbor by then and gave no sign of quitting or turning around. The bartender kept rowing.

By the time we caught up with him he was halfway to Angel Island and the powerful current running through Raccoon Straits was pulling him way off course. He was still fully dressed but had kicked off his sneakers, and when I leaned over the side and tried grabbing his collar he ducked under the water like an otter and came up on the other side and started swimming again, so we circled around him and tried heading him off. I finally managed to get a good hold on his hair and he let out a yell, but I hung on and wouldn't let go. He kept thrashing and trying to duck down again but I yanked on his hair really hard and the son of a bitch stopped struggling. We hauled him into the dinghy and rowed back to Tiburon without saying a word. We were all shivering, of course, and the whitecaps felt like hail. Al's collar was almost torn off and I noticed a very long scratch on the side of his neck.

An ambulance was waiting. He climbed in and somebody handed him one of his birthday presents and the ambulance took off for Marin General, and that's the last time I saw him. I understand the hospital kept him overnight for observation and he took the bus back to the city the next day and packed an overnight bag while I was out jogging with Colleen and flew off to New York.

I don't know how he's doing on Long Island Sound and I don't especially want to find out, it's just taken too much out of me. I guess we never really talked the same language. Things were fine when we were running around doing meaningful things and he was wearing all those hats, but the pressures were always inside him and I could never understand why he couldn't release them somehow. I don't know if he's ever going to finish that book or if he'll get the real answer about his father or if he'll ever get over the misery of being so short. I don't think he'll come back to the West Coast—he was never really happy out here.